Starcrossed

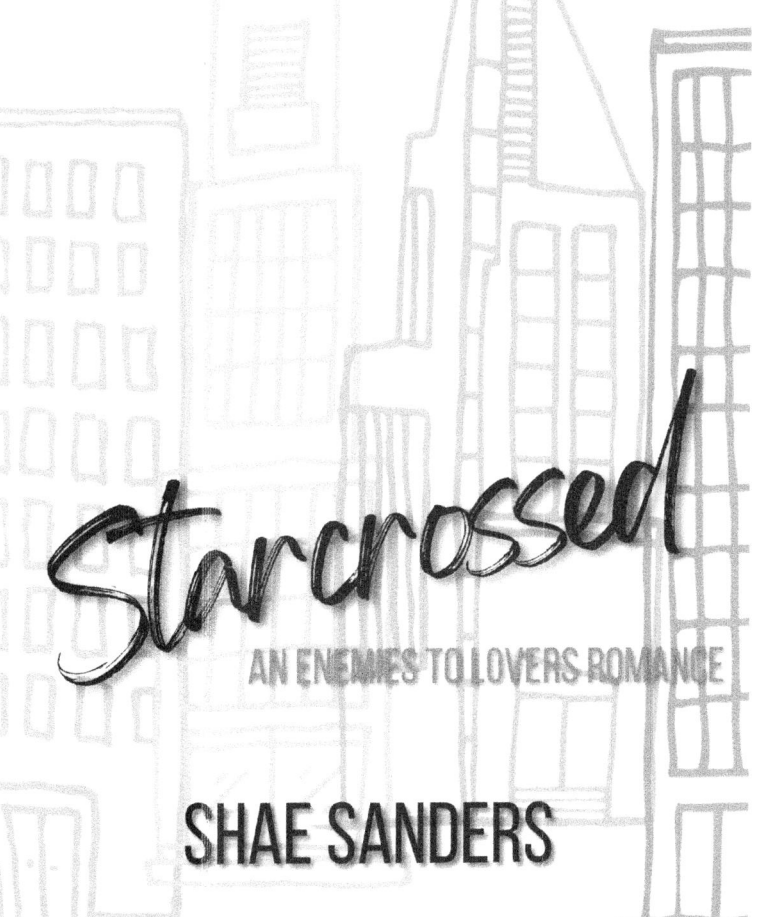

AN ENEMIES TO LOVERS ROMANCE

SHAE SANDERS

Copyright © 2024 Shae Sanders

All rights reserved.

No portion of this book may be reproduced in any form without written permission from the publisher or author, except as permitted by U.S. copyright law.

Contents

Author's Note	1
1. Electra	2
2. Vic	5
3. Electra	11
4. Vic	18
5. Electra	22
6. Vic	29
7. Electra	37
8. Vic	43
9. Electra	48
10. Vic	51
11. Electra	55
12. Vic	60
13. Electra	63
14. Vic	67

15.	Electra	71
16.	Vic	77
17.	Electra	79
18.	Vic	83
19.	Electra	90
20.	Electra	98
21.	Vic	106
22.	Electra	114
23.	Vic	119
24.	Electra	127
25.	Vic	134
26.	Electra	141
27.	Vic	144
28.	Electra	148
29.	Vic	155
30.	Vic	164
31.	Electra	172
32.	Vic	179
33.	Electra	187
34.	Vic	191
35.	Electra	196
36.	Electra	201
37.	Epilogue	207

Thank You	210
About the Author	211
Books by Shae Sanders	212

Author's Note

This is book 2 in the Jackson Brothers series. It's not vital that you read the previous book, *The Replacements*, but you'll enjoy this one more if you do.

Please be advised that this story contains profanity, explicit sex, and very brief mention of miscarriage.

Love, Shae

1

Electra

I was about to go to war.

As such, I donned my battle gear. Crisp white blouse. Black pencil skirt. Black blazer. Wolford stockings. Black patent leather heels. "Outer perfection begets inner success," my mother would always say, and I'd always sought to prove that statement was true.

Thanks to Lola squeezing me in yesterday evening, my hair had joined my clothes in the pursuit of perfection. She'd tortured my coily strands into a sleek shoulder-length bob. I had to beg and plead for time in her chair, but it was worth it. I'm not usually so last-minute with things, but it wasn't my fault. I got the call from StarTech just yesterday morning.

I rushed out the front door of my apartment, grabbing my snakeskin attaché case on the way. No time for Starbucks today, but that was fine. I'd get my usual after the meeting. To celebrate.

This was going to be the day I got a win.

Lord knows I deserved it.

Thirteen hard-fought years in the consulting industry had wrung me out, but a victory today would make it all worth it. I could simultaneously solidify my company's place among the best firms in the southeast, and maybe, just maybe, restore my good name once and for all.

But if I lost?

I was going to have to start over. At thirty-six years old.

Twenty minutes later, I hurried through the door of StarTech's newly constructed office building. They'd only been open here in Summerville for about six months, and I know that because the construction made it extremely difficult for me to get to favorite yoga studio.

The pretty receptionist at the sleek glass desk smiled as I approached.

"Hi. Electra Montrose here for a meeting with—"

"Yes, Ms. Montrose. They're ready for you," she said. "Fifth floor conference room. Would like me to escort you?"

"That's okay…Kelly," I said, reading her name plate. "I can find it. Thanks so much."

A deep breath. Then another. The mirrored elevator doors offered me a chance to stare at myself. I flashed a smile. I'd never really worried about my reflection. She had her shit together. I made sure of it.

I couldn't always say the same for the woman on the other side.

I stepped off at the ding and stared straight ahead at the sign on the wall, which told me the conference room was to the right.

Various voices filled my ears as I approached the door, most of them parroting corporate speak in soulless tones that didn't run the risk of giving offense.

This was my element.

Squaring my shoulders, I rounded the corner like a model on a catwalk, striding with purpose and style, determined to make my presence known to every other consultant sitting in that room.

I'm that bitch.

I got this.

But when I walked in and spotted *him*, we locked eyes and I stopped and froze as everything around me disappeared.

He looked exactly the same as he did twelve years ago when I first saw him. I remember marveling at his bone structure that day; the strong jaw, chiseled cheek bones, and sturdy chin, the totality of which gave male model more than business consultant.

The first words he ever said to me were, "How you doin'? I'm Victor Jackson. I'll probably be your boss one day."

Despite the deep, gravelly timbre of his voice, and the shivers it sent through me, his words—joke or not—turned me completely off. From that day on, I was on the defense. Good thing, too, given what he ultimately did to me.

And there he was. Twelve years later. Older, but still unfairly handsome. His forehead creased as his eyebrows raised in surprise, but he covered quickly, his face going blank.

Not that I expected it, but there was no warmth. No smile. No curiosity. Just cold, hard resolve.

Well, two could play that game.

2

VIC

IT WAS *HER*.

Involuntarily, I straightened my back at the sight of her, having forgotten the conversation I'd just been engaged in with Andrew, StarTech's operations manager.

Yeah, fuck Andrew.

This was serious.

Electra Montrose. Electra *Fucking* Montrose.

I hadn't seen her in over ten years. And thank God for that, because she was the most manipulative, vindictive, treacherous woman I'd ever had the misfortune of knowing.

If I'd been aware that she was in the mix today, I would have been more prepared. The woman was as smart as she was shady.

She strutted in like she owned the fucking place. Eyes followed her every move just like they did back then, because unlike the inside, the outside of her was beautiful. Perfect hair, makeup, clothes. And she was wearing these stockings, or pantyhose, or...I don't know the difference. All I know is I stared at them, watching the lace dance as her legs moved.

Then they stopped.

I looked up, my eyes locking on hers. She looked dazed, like she'd just seen a handsome ghost. But just as quick as she froze up, she thawed again, continuing her approach until Jason, another StarTech exec, pointed her to her seat.

Well, then.

The day just got interesting.

I realized something as my eyes darted around the full conference room. When I got yesterday's call to come back in for a final Q&A session with myself and a few other finalists, I didn't think much about it. That happens all the time in this industry. Nobody *gives* you their business; you have to win it.

I just didn't think *she'd* be one of my rivals.

And now that the conference room was full, it was dawning on me that we were the last two standing. It was a cruel twist of fate given our past, but fuck it. I had a job to do. Well, two.

The *primary* job was to win the client. But giving Electra Montrose a professional ass-whoopin' was a very close second.

Carter Wells, a smug frat boy type wearing an ill-fitting suit, smiled big as he looked back and forth between us.

"Welcome, both of you. We're so glad you could make it back today."

He said that like we had any choice in the matter. This had the potential to be a half-million-dollar account. Our black asses were making it back today.

"Of course," I said. "I'm—"

"I'm so grateful for the opportunity!" she said over me.

Already on her bullshit.

I kept my eyes on Carter's. "As she said, I appreciate the opportunity."

His eyes shone with amusement. "Well, it came down to the two of you. We were very impressed. So impressed, we needed one last round to properly evaluate your companies."

Me and her.

Overtime.

Sudden death.

StarTech was in the middle of a southern expansion, and they'd chosen our sleepy little town to do it in. They were looking to gain a foothold in autonomous vehicle technology, or, in simpler terms, self-driving cars. It was all very preliminary, and this project was the absolute first drop in a very large bucket. But if it went well, it would be the start of something major. For me, and for them.

Katie, StarTech's HR manager, tapped in from the other end of the table. "Electra, let's start with you."

Ladies first.

Fine with me.

"How do you tackle project management on this scale?"

That was a softball. Electra knew it, too, which is why she smiled. It was irritating how pretty she was, because her beauty made it way too easy to forget she was a shark. Even worse, it was exactly the kind of pretty I liked...the brown-skinned, Barbie type.

"My approach is about precision and agility," she said. "I believe in thorough planning coupled with a readiness to pivot when necessary. It's all about staying ahead of the curve and ensuring seamless execution."

I didn't try to hide my smirk as I listened to the words pour out of her heart-shaped mouth. *That's* what she came up with? All these years, and she still talked like a robot.

All eyes shifted to me.

"Precision is all well and good," I said, "but I prefer a more collaborative approach."

Electra cut her eyes at me, but I continued. "It's not just about the plan; it's about empowering the team to think creatively and adapt on the fly. Flexibility is key."

"Which is why I mentioned readiness to pivot," she snapped.

"Right. Which is reactive. Flexibility is *proactive*. StarTech is a cutting edge tech outfit that's breaking into a market that's currently dominated by Tesla, so I don't think they have time to sit around waiting for you to come up with a plan for your little pivoting strategy."

If looks could kill.

In any other context, her stare would have come off sultry. Those big, brown, almond-shaped eyes, those long lashes that curved up at the corners. Any man would find that enticing.

But not me.

Not today, anyway.

"Thank you," Andrew said. "Victor, we'll stick with you. How do you handle conflicts within a team setting?"

Simple.

"Good question, Andrew. Conflict resolution is an art, really. I approach it with empathy and finesse, always striving to find common ground with team members. It's about fostering a culture of trust and communication. That's especially important in your industry. Innovation never occurs without conflict."

"True indeed." He looked over at Electra. "And you?"

She smiled. "I agree with him, but I have to say, I'm surprised he didn't mention conflict *prevention*, given his stated preference for proactive strategy. I believe it's about setting clear expectations and holding everyone accountable. I don't see the need to sugarcoat it with finesse."

Her eyes shifted to me. "Maybe I'm just more aggressive than Mr. Jackson."

Andrew's eyebrows raised slowly as murmurs raced quietly around the room.

"Thank you. Um, let's see..." he trailed off, flipping through his papers. "Ah, okay. Victor, how do you ensure your recommendations align with our long-term goals?"

"Well, as you know from my pitch, I have an extensive tech background. But I'm also a student of your company. I immersed myself in StarTech's vision and strategy." I paused to look around the room. "Not to get too deep into buzzword territory, but as your consultant, I would tailor bespoke solutions that synergize with your digital transformation roadmap. It's about becoming an integral part of your ecosystem, not just a hired hand."

Electra chuckled. "I feel like I've heard that somewhere before."

"I'm sure you have. I've spoken at several conferences."

She snapped her fingers. "Conferences! That's probably it." She smiled at the others. "Well, while he was busy speaking, I was *working*, and in the course of my work, I gained valuable experience embedding myself within the organizational DNA of various clients."

"Small clients," I muttered.

"Anyway, that's really the only way to truly understand. I use continuous feedback loops and KPIs to facilitate adaptive strategy execution. I'm dynamic. Never static. And that's exactly what you need."

For the first time since she walked in, I started to doubt that I'd win this one.

After a few more rounds of questions, Carter cleared his throat, then plastered on a smile. "Thank you both for your... spirited responses. If you don't mind, I'd like to ask you to step out for a bit to let us deliberate. We'll let you know our decision shortly."

"No problem," Electra said. "And—"

"Thank you for your consideration," I said. "I look forward to hearing your decision."

She cut her eyes at me, following closely behind me as I exited the room.

Outside in the narrow hallway, we positioned ourselves on opposite walls like two heroes in a country western. I didn't know who would draw first or who would emerge victorious, but I was sure of one thing: it was gonna be bloody.

In the conference room, she was all big and bad. Out here, up close and personal, she refused to look at me. With her eyes glued to her cell phone screen, she blocked me out. I didn't exist.

Something about that really pissed me off.

Maybe it was because she'd always been like that with me, even way back when we first got hired on at Nexus. With her nose to the sky, she judged me and everybody else who dared to breathe her precious air. She was Ivy; I was HBCU. She was pedigreed; I was first generation middle class. Only things we had in common were being black, sexy, and new to the consulting business.

So it shouldn't have come as a surprise when she fucked me over. I was still cleaning up that mess. Still trying to restore my name. The fact that we were both still in the running for an account this major was a miracle.

But I like to think I'm one of God's favorites.

My tongue practically itched from the urge to say something to her. Something mean. Song lyrics filled my head just then.

And if you're wondering if I hate you...
FUUUUUCK YOOOOOU

Bless SZA for singing a nigga's feelings.

But the way I was feeling, I was probably gonna need something stronger. Pac. Nas. Kendrick.

Her eyes flipped up suddenly like a reptile and landed on my face. For several seconds, it was like an optical tug of war in this bitch, neither of us letting go of the thing between us, both of us yanking and tugging, hoping to knock the other off balance. But no dice. We were both so strong, we canceled each other out.

Eyes burning, I held that stare. I couldn't let her win this one after she'd damn near cooked me in the Q&A.

Those pretty eyes looked through me. I held the line though, until I couldn't anymore.

I blinked.

On her shiny pink lips, I thought I saw a hint of a smirk, but I couldn't swear to it in a court of law. If it were true, it let me know in no uncertain terms that no matter what happened in that conference room when they called us back, this was war.

3

Electra

He was still irritatingly fine.

For a man in his late 30s, he was surprisingly fit. He could pass for a college basketball player, in fact. Golden brown skin, piercing brown eyes, and a smoldering gaze which, in any other context, would make my panties melt off. But right now?

It was maddening.

The hallway wasn't big, but there were plenty of other places for him to look besides my face. Passing over the floor and ceiling and the generic pastoral paintings lining the walls to ogle me was a definite choice.

I stared right back. Unflinching. I never back down from a fight. It's just how I was raised. The illustrious Montrose family didn't birth quitters.

When he blinked, I felt an internal charge. Even if I lost in there, I won out here.

"Victor? Electra? You can come back in now."

Both of us looked away just then. Saved by a bell named Andrew.

I followed Victor in—*such* a gentleman, walking in front of me like that. The smiling faces around the conference table made me uneasy. They weren't let-you-down-easy smiles, which one of us should have been getting. They were triumphant smiles.

Something was afoot.

We retook our seats and waited without sparing another look at one another.

"We've come to a decision. I'd say it was difficult, but I don't like to lie."

Laughs sounded around the table.

"It's pretty simple," Andrew continued. "We'd like to bring you both in as contractors. We feel that you each bring something unique that compliments the other."

"Oh," I said softly. "That's..."

"What do you mean when you say, 'together?'" Victor interrupted.

"You'll work in tandem. You'll be assigned a liaison from StarTech to make sure there's synergy, but make no mistake, this will be a joint effort between your two companies."

I swallowed hard as the news penetrated.

"I'm not sure I understand," I said, trying my hardest to maintain my composure. "My hiring is contingent upon my willingness to work with…Victor?"

"I wouldn't say your willingness. More like, your *ability*."

Well, that was loud and clear.

It wasn't unprecedented in the industry. Neither of us could play dumb about that. It was just…impossible. Us working together was going to be a disaster. I couldn't even picture it in my mind.

"Listen. It's no secret that you worked together before," Andrew continued. "Word gets around."

I nodded.

"We're not interested in that. It was the past. We're interested in what we saw in your pitches, and in your Q&A today. Iron sharpening iron."

I glanced at Lucifer. His tight jaw and furrowed brow let me know he was just as conflicted about this as I was, although likely for a very different reason.

I looked around at StarTech's staff and wondered if he even noticed I was only one of two women in the room. I know he noticed we were only two of the three black faces around the table. Both the tech and consulting fields could be hostile places for people like us, but I got it double. Well, triple. I'm black, a woman, and a black woman. The third is its own identity.

Not that he should bow out and let me have this, but...I kinda wanted him to bow out and let me have this.

"We'll give you a day to decide," Katie said. "Clock starts now."

Quiet laughter sounded around the table, but I knew it wasn't a joke. One day.

That was all the time I had to decide if I wanted to work with my mortal enemy.

First thing I did when I got in my car was call my best friend. If anyone could make me feel better about an impossible situation, it was her.

"Hey, can I call you back?" was her breathless greeting. "I'm about to have sex."

But only when I was able to get past her unseriousness.

"It's important, Ci."

"So is my orgasm."

"Ciara!"

"Okay, okay. Give me one second."

I heard muffled voices and the distinct rustling of clothes. I didn't feel bad about interrupting her, because Lord knows she'd done it to me before. Last time I was about to go to pound town with Lance, here she came blowing up my phone because her dog and cat got into a fight.

"Alright, what's wrong?"

I blew out a sigh. "If you had a chance to work on a half a million-dollar account, would you do it?"

"Barring exigent circumstances, um, hell yeah."

Of course that was her answer. Ci loved money. It was why she majored in finance in the first place despite being horrible at math. I was proud of her, though. That undergrad accounting class almost made her quit altogether, but now she was a wealth manager with Citibank. Money was her reason for waking up in the morning.

"What if you had to work with your sworn enemy?" I qualified.

"Sworn enemy?" She laughed. "Bitch, you in a Marvel movie now?"

"Victor Jackson."

"Oh, shit."

She was quiet for a while, as was I. My eyes shifted to the scene before me, filtered through the yellow pollen on my dashboard. Trees swaying gently in a light breeze. People walking to and from the office building, smiling and laughing with their work friends. Cars easing through the parking lot. Such an ordinary day for everyone but me. I was living a nightmare.

"What should I do?"

"Get money," she said. "That's what you do."

"I don't wanna work with him again."

"I know, but StarTech is a big deal, El. This is what you've been working towards. You gonna let all that go over one man?"

"One man who almost ruined my career."

"Right, so are you gonna give him a *second* chance to ruin you? Or are you gonna walk up in there like the bad bitch you are and make that negro regret the day he got on your bad side?"

"I don't trust him."

"Nor should you. But this time, you know he ain't shit out the gate. You're prepared. It's a whole different situation now."

I took a deep breath. "You know what? You're right."

"When am I not?"

"Um…you want a list, or do you wanna get off the phone and get some D."

"I'll call you tomorrow, girl. Love you. You got this."

"Love you, too."

Just as I was driving off, a call came through. Being the responsible driver that I am, I pulled over and put the car in park.

Private number.

All I could think was, this better not be *him*.

"This is Electra."

"Electra, hello! This is Nora Brown. I've been assigned as your liaison on the consulting project."

"Hi. Yes, I haven't actually given my answer on that yet."

"That's why I'm calling. I certainly don't want to rush you, but this is a time-sensitive project, and the team can't pause operations while they wait for a response."

I nodded to myself. It was reasonable. *We'll give you a day* was their way of being polite.

"Has the other party given their answer already?"

"Yes..." she trailed off, which told me that was all I was gonna get from her.

"Okay. My answer is yes."

"Perfect. Now, given the scope of this project, the team thought it was important for you and Mr. Jackson to come out to the New York office."

"Really? Okay. When?"

"Tomorrow."

"That's...fast."

"Yes. I understand."

Her silence let me know it wasn't negotiable, so I squared my shoulders and said, "Sounds good! Can't wait to meet the rest of the team."

And with any luck, I'd outshine my enemy.

There are only two people at my company. Me and a virtual assistant whose face I've never seen. And only one partner. Me. As such, Horizons Consulting wasn't important enough to worry about the head possibly dying in a plane crash. One of my dreams was to grow us to the eventual point where I had partners, and we'd be flying on separate flights just in case.

That would mean I'd made it.

And that I could finally shut my family up.

I made it through airport security, then grabbed my Starbucks on the way to the gate. The email confirmation had both mine and Victor's information on it, so I said a quick prayer that the third person seated in our row got stuck in traffic. There was no way I was gonna feel comfortable sitting right next to *him* for almost four hours.

I found a seat at the gate and sat, taking a hot sip of espresso as my eyes flickered over the people around me. A mother consoling a small child. Two teenage girls giggling over something on a phone screen. A man walking by with the most adorable little service dog. I said *awww* in my head just before Beelzebub came into my view.

I averted my eyes, but it was too late.

All six feet of him sauntered towards me like I was an old friend, rather than a mortal enemy. His blue jeans fit him like a male model. His

Howard hoodie did nothing to hide his impressive upper body. It was a shame he was such a lying scumbag. Objectively speaking, the man was *fine*.

He stopped a few feet away, then changed direction. I didn't see where he went, nor did I look, because I was not about to give him the satisfaction of knowing I cared about his location. So I stared straight ahead and finished my drink.

I boarded first. Row one, which was great, but I had the middle seat, which was not. Anyone else, and I would have asked for the window seat, but asking *him* for a favor?

Never.

I refused to even look at him when he stopped at our row, although my peripheral vision betrayed me when he lifted his arms to put his bag in the overhead compartment. That Bison hoodie, and the white t-shirt underneath, lifted just enough to show a strip of golden brown skin on his abdomen.

Why didn't he tuck his t-shirt in?

So annoying.

"Excuse me."

Before I could react, two long legs climbed over me. A fresh, clean scent wafted into my nose. Then he was seated, and I reiterated my prayer for the person next to me not to show up.

No such luck. My other seatmate arrived and flopped down in a huff. I stared down at my vibrating phone.

Lance

> **Can I see you tonight?**

A slow smile spread across my face.

> **I'm on my way to NY. Raincheck?**

> **Of course. I'll miss you. You gonna miss me?**

> **Maybe**

"Boyfriend?"

I instinctively turned my head toward the prince of darkness despite my determination to ignore him for the next three days.

"Excuse me?"

"You smilin' all in the phone. Boyfriend, right?"

It seemed like his eyes lit up when I finally looked at him.

"How is that your business?"

He shrugged. "It's not, but I had to break the ice some kinda way."

"You really didn't."

"Yeah, I did. This is a half-million-dollar account, and we have a babysitter. We both need to get over ourselves so we can get this bag."

I rolled my eyes at that.

His flashed with anger. "Trust me, I don't wanna work with you any more than you wanna work with me."

"The last thing I'd ever do is trust you."

"Well, you don't have a choice, do you?"

I turned my head back to the front and scooted as far as I could to my left. Which was about a centimeter.

I didn't like it, but he was on broken-clock status today.

I didn't have a choice.

4

VIC

Taurus

Bruh.

> I know, man. I was going today but they got me headed to NY

I need your measurements

> Soon as I get back

When is that? Savannah's on my ass

> My bad. I'm back on Thursday

Nah. You gotta find a tailor or something while you're up there. You're holding shit up

> Ain't we bout the same height and size? Just give 'em yours

> Nigga take yo ass to a tailor by tomorrow or this woman gon leave me

I SNICKERED AT MY brother's antics. Him and his fiancée were set to be married in a couple of months, and he was insufferable these days—even more than usual. He was happy, but he was stressed, and somehow, that was all my fault.

Okay, I *did* procrastinate on getting my measurements taken, but still. I was running a business. He of all people should have understood that.

"Girlfriend?"

I set my phone on my lap and looked over at the beautiful she-beast sitting beside me.

"Tit for tat? That's what we doin'?"

"Just returning the favor," she said with a shrug.

"If I didn't know any better, I'd think you cared."

"Good thing you know better."

I stared at her perfect profile and wondered if she remembered turning me down for a date.

It was the very first day we met. We were both brand new at Nexus. She was cute, and we were both single, so I decided to shoot my shot.

I didn't know at the time how uptight and by-the-book she was. According to her, we couldn't...what were her exact words?

"As the only two black employees on the team, I don't think we can afford the appearance of impropriety. I'm flattered, but I'm afraid I have to decline."

I remember staring at her, confused as hell, because she really could have kept all that extra bullshit. 'No' would have sufficed.

So that's the fucking foot we got off on. Corny as hell right out the gate. I was good on her after that. Uptight ass.

She'd changed a little since then, though. Back then, she was girl-next-door cute. Fresh-faced and young, she had an innocence about her. Now, though? Grown ass woman. Mysterious. Sexy. Polished. I wasn't sure what changed, but it was working for her.

But that was for some other man to enjoy.

After takeoff, I pulled out my laptop and got to work. That was the goal, anyway. I wanted a running start on this project. StarTech wasn't fucking around.

But it was hard to stay focused.

The sun was blazing bright on my right side. The succubus smelled like honey on my left. What the fuck even *was* that? Who walks around smelling like honey? Shit was distracting.

The flight tracker told me we had a little over three hours before we reached our destination.

If I couldn't get any work done, I was gonna have to amuse myself somehow.

I looked over at her. "We have to talk at some point."

Without taking her eyes off her phone, she shrugged a shoulder. "Doesn't have to be right now, does it?"

"Probably better to do it now when there's nowhere to run."

That got her eyes on me. Second time today, and it was already getting old. When she looked at me, it was lowkey exhilarating, and I wasn't interested in that.

"Why would I run?" she said. "You think I'm scared of you?"

"Fear has nothing to do with it. We can't stand each other."

"First time you've been right," she said.

"Whatever. I'm trying to get this money. I need to know you can put your animosity to the side for both of our sakes."

"Can *you*?"

"Why are you answering a question with a question?"

"You didn't ask a question. You said you need to know. That's a statement."

Still a fucking piece of work.

Through gritted teeth, I said, "*Can you* put all your bullshit to the side for the money's sake? Yes or no?"

Electra didn't have a poker face. At least not with me. Her lips pursed, and her whole demeanor changed like she was personally offended that she had to answer to me.

"What does that look like to you?" she said.

"What, putting your bullshit to the side?"

She nodded, but even her nod had extra attitude.

"It means we can be cordial," I said. "Put on a united front for the client. Be professional."

She took a long pause. For what, I don't know. Didn't look like she was thinking. She looked more like she was plotting. But finally, she muttered, "I can agree to that."

"What did you *think* I meant?"

"Doesn't matter," she snapped. "And don't ask me to shake on it. I don't wanna touch you."

"Aye, I wasn't gonna ask. When I touch a woman, I like her to feel soft, not cold and brittle."

Her right eye twitched just before she gave me an exaggerated shrug. I'd found another tell.

She mumbled something.

"What'd you say?"

She sighed. "I *said* I'm not cold and brittle. I'm very soft with people who deserve it."

I started to ask her what it took to deserve it, but then I remembered I didn't give a fuck about that. So instead, I forced out a laugh.

"That's funny?"

"Yeah. I can't picture it. At all."

She turned her nose up. "Good. I don't *want* you picturing me. In any capacity."

"Don't flatter yourself, sweetheart."

I said that shit, but the truth was, as soon as she said it, the picturing started. It was like a switch had flipped my internal light on. My shit was flashing.

Clear as day, I saw her in that black suit from the other day. Face clear and smooth. Legs long and shapely, and covered with those fucking stockings. I wasn't sure what it was about them, but they caught my eye. They were seared into my brain.

And for a brief moment, I imagined myself touching her. I imagined the softness she'd just mentioned. I could practically feel the silk of her skin against my fingertips, and hear the softness in her voice, and feel it in her attitude towards me. I almost closed my eyes to let a movie play out in my head, one in which I made a home in *all* of her softness, but then I remembered I couldn't stand this woman and came back to my senses.

There was no time for that.

And even if there was, she was the wrong fucking one.

5

ELECTRA

"New York? What on earth are you doing in New York?"

I plopped down on the queen bed in my hotel room and crossed my legs into an easy pose, bracing myself for this conversation. "I'm working, Mama."

The remainder of the plane ride was fine, mostly because Victor stopped talking to me. Deplaning was smooth. Taxiing to the hotel and check-in were both seamless. But this phone call with my mother?

My shoulders were already tight.

"I just don't understand why you didn't want to talk to that law firm I mentioned to you awhile back."

"Because I'm not a lawyer?"

"No, to *sue*."

"Who would I sue?"

"That company!"

I sighed. "We've been over this. Several times. They were within their legal rights to terminate my contract."

She took a deep breath, and I braced myself again. The Nexus situation was always a sore subject between us.

"Well, be that as it may, at least give the *appearance* that you didn't go down without a fight."

Ah, yes. Those all-important appearances.

I pinched the bridge of my nose. "That's not why I called you, Mama. I was calling you back about Daddy's birthday."

She let out an embarrassed chuckle. "I...well, I wasn't really calling you about that. I know I mentioned it in the voicemail, but I was mostly calling you about your brother. We need to know if you're coming to the anniversary."

I'd been putting off answering, but of *course* I was going to the anniversary of Redeemer's Path Baptist Church, home of senior paster Emory Montrose, the one child my parents were proud of.

Just like StarTech, I didn't have a choice in the matter.

"I'll be there," I said on an exhale. "I'm not sure my presence will make a difference, though."

"He's getting an award," she said proudly. "There will be lots of pictures. You need to be there."

"Award for what?"

"Excellence in Ministry."

I bit back a laugh. "And who's presenting this award?"

"Why do you do that?"

"What?"

"Downplay other people's achievements?"

"I don't."

That was *her* wheelhouse, not mine.

"To answer your question, I don't exactly know who's giving the award. But it's a big deal, Electra."

"I said I'll be there."

"And listen, if or when *you* win something, we will all be there to cheer you on."

I didn't respond to that. To do so would be as futile as catching wind in a net.

"So...about Daddy's birthday..."

"Oh, that's still a couple of months away. We'll deal with that when it's looming."

I sighed. "Okay, then, Mama. It was nice talking to you."

"Wait! Tell me about this New York job thing. That's new."

A quick internal debate revealed that there was no good argument for telling her about any of it, so I simply said, "I'm hoping to win a new client," and left it at that.

The lie made me thirsty, and not for water. I stepped into my Born loafers and grabbed my tote before heading down to the hotel bar. I probably should have dressed a bit nicer given the fact that it was a fancy New York hotel and all, but that conversation had drained me of my last shred of energy. These skinny jeans were gonna have to do for tonight.

I stepped off the elevator and entered the bar area. Shiny marble caught my footfalls as ornate chandeliers drew my eyes up high. The place looked both expensive and exclusive, which I took to mean that it was perfect for me.

Gassing myself is my favorite past time.

I rounded the corner, passing off a smile to the cute bartender before freezing where I stood. *He* was there, sitting at the bar, laughing with some woman, and I felt a strange sensation at the sight of it.

I was bothered.

Ciara would say I'm bothered by a lot of things, and she would be absolutely right. I can be uptight occasionally, if occasionally means daily. But only about things that are my concern. Victor Jackson wasn't my concern at all, so why did I have such a visceral reaction to this?

I put a hand on the plush black velvet bar stool next to me and practically fell onto it, hoping he hadn't seen me. I kept my body facing forward, bringing my eyes up to the flatscreen on the wall. Somebody was playing basketball. Seemed interesting. I stared blankly, understanding nothing as my heart thudded in my chest.

Then I heard footsteps. His voice moving closer. I clenched my fists, or maybe they clenched themselves. All I know is by the time he made it to my side with that woman in tow, my acrylic nails felt like they were going to pop off.

"Is this her?" the woman asked.

I turned my head toward them.

"This is Electra," he said, his eyes flickering over me. "Electra, this is Nora. She's the liaison StarTech sent to babysit—I mean *work* with us."

The silly laugh Nora expelled just then told me they were familiar. She even went so far as to lightly slap him on the shoulder. A playful *boy stop* gesture.

I looked her over, making a quick assessment that calmed me down. She was older than us by at least fifteen years. Fifteen *kind* years, that is.

Time had left its marks on her face, but they added a mature, regal touch to her beauty.

I forced myself to smile. "Nora, it's so nice to meet you."

I stuck out my hand and she shook it, giving me a warm, inviting grin.

"You, as well. I feel like I know you already."

"Really?"

"Yes. Victor told me quite a bit about you."

My eyes narrowed, but I refused to give him the satisfaction of watching me puzzle that out. So I simply said, "Good things, I hope. I'd love to hear about you, Nora."

She nodded and took the seat next to me. Victor sat on her other side and listened as Nora talked my ear off about things he'd probably already heard before I got here. Like the fact that she was married with three children. She also described her long career in the industry, floating from city to city until she landed at StarTech's New York office.

She was starting to tell me about her responsibilities on our current project when the bartender finally got tired of waiting.

"Drinks, ladies?"

Nora nodded. "Pina Colada. Light on the rum, please."

I smiled at that. She wasn't quite old enough, but she reminded me of my mother with that one.

The bartender turned to me, but before I could speak, Victor said, "Oh, none for her. She's sober."

I whipped my head to the left and glared. "Why would you say it like that?"

His smirk infuriated me. "If I recall correctly, you don't drink."

One time.

I turned down a drink *one time* at a dinner for the new hires at Nexus. That was twelve whole years ago that I refused that drink, and it was only because I needed to keep a clear head and stay professional in front of our boss. How the hell did he even remember that?

"I drink occasionally," I corrected. "And when you say somebody's sober, it implies they're an alcoholic."

"Does it? I didn't know," he said, like butter wouldn't melt in his mouth.

I turned back to Chris, our bartender. "*Anyway*, I'll have a dry white. The driest you have."

"Sauvignon Blanc okay?"

"Perfect." I turned to Nora. "Don't mind Victor. He hates drinking alone. You know how those types can be."

Nora chuckled at that. "I do, indeed."

"Wow. Okay," he said, then he took the rest of his drink to the head as if to punctuate that. "You ladies are already ganging up on me. Lemme put the number to HR in my contacts. I see I'ma need some protection around you two."

Nora threw her head back and laughed. "Is he always like this?" she said to me.

I locked eyes with Victor, annoyed that he seemed to be enjoying this, and that Nora seemed so charmed by him.

"Not all the time," I said. "Sometimes he's serious. Those are the times you have to watch out."

"Oh?" Nora's eyes sparkled with mischief. "Watch out for what?"

"Oh, not in a bad way," I rushed out. "Victor's like a wolf. When he wants something, it doesn't matter what, or *who,* is standing in his way."

"Well those are good traits in this business," she said.

"Rather be a wolf than a snake," he muttered as he signaled Chris and slid his glass across the bar. "Another."

Thirty minutes and lots of friendly conversation—with Nora—later, she pushed her empty glass away and stood.

"Well." She checked her phone. "I have to get back to the office to finish up. It was wonderful meeting you two. Do you have your itineraries?"

We both nodded.

"Perfect. Shall I close you out?"

"I got it," Victor said. "I'm sure we'll do this again."

She nodded. "I'll see you both tomorrow. Bright and early!"

The vacuum she left in her wake was palpable, as was the shift in the atmosphere. Only about twelve inches separated me and Lucifer, but thank goodness for them. I wanted no parts.

Chris, the bartender, brought me a club soda, like I asked. "Enjoy," he said with a wink.

I smiled back and took a sip, taking great care to keep my body, head, and eyes forward.

When Chris returned with Victor's third drink, he passed in front of me, locking eyes with me to wink again.

Not very subtle, but I appreciated the energy.

"He's choosin'."

I rolled my eyes at the sound of my new coworker's deep, annoying voice. "So?"

"You gonna give him your number?"

"Why do you care?"

"I don't. I'm just entertaining myself."

"Well there's a game on. Surely that's more entertaining than worrying about me and what I do."

"I can't multitask?"

I took another sip, sighing as the tension made a home in my body. Again.

Victor cleared his throat. "I could have sworn we agreed to put on a united front for the client."

"We did."

"You seem to be struggling with that."

I set my glass on the mahogany bar and swiveled until my whole body faced him. "What does that mean?"

"It means I talked you up to the client before you got here, but you couldn't seem to do the same."

"First of all, I didn't get a chance. And second...what exactly did you say about me?"

"You don't trust that I can say nice things about you?" He smirked. "I know how to lie."

My eyes dropped to his full lips, lingering there just long enough for me to bet myself that he was a good kisser. I quickly shoved that thought out of my mind.

"What did you tell her about me?"

He took another pull from his drink, then set it down slowly. *Too* slowly. It felt like he was deliberately putting on a show. Even worse, the audience—me—was riveted. His long-sleeved shirt was a little too formfitting for my taste, hugging his arms and shoulders and chest in an almost vulgar way. Disgusted, I watched his forearm extend out, then retract and come to rest at his side, muscles flexing all the way.

He really could have done that faster and less...*peacocky*.

His eyes locked on mine. "I told her you're smart. Sharp. Professional. Insightful. Creative. And that you do what it takes for the client. All the cliches. All the bullshit."

"Well…thanks, I guess."

He shrugged a shoulder. "Like I said, I know how to lie."

I turned away from him then, completely uninterested in his hostility. My eyes returned to the television as I finished my soda and pretended I wasn't moved by what he'd just said.

It's not that I cared about his raggedy opinion. I was simply surprised he was able to even muster up something positive. I also wondered if he actually believed those things about me. I definitely believed them about myself. Most of the time.

I pulled a twenty out of my wallet and set it on the bar next to my empty glass.

"I got it."

I stood and grabbed my tote, looking at Victor one last time to say, "No thanks," before leaving him alone at the bar.

The last thing I wanted was to owe him anything.

6

Vic

I shouldn't have drank so much yesterday.

My pounding head woke me before my alarm. I knew I needed to get up, but I lay there with my eyes squeezed shut, hoping the marching band inside my head would stop stomping around up there.

I opened my eyes at the sound of my ringing phone. I already knew who it would be before I even looked at the screen.

My fucking brother.

"No, I didn't go yet," was my greeting. "I just got here."

I heard him take a deep breath.

"Lemme tell you something, Vic. You not gon' fuck this up for me."

"It ain't that deep, bruh."

"It's my fucking wedding."

"Number *two*," I mumbled.

He laughed, and it was a strange sound coming from him. Like playing two dissonant chords on an old fucked up piano. "Don't hate, Vic. I got *two* women to marry me. What you got?"

"Fuck you."

"Yeah. Aye, take yo' ass to the—"

"I am!"

"Today."

"Yes, nigga. Today." I sat up and stretched, grimacing as a bomb went off inside my skull. "You act like you the only one with shit goin' on."

"What you got goin' on?"

"I got StarTech."

"You got it? That's a big deal. Congrats, Vic. I'm proud of you."

"Guess who I'm working with."

"Now you know I ain't into no guessing games."

"Remember ol' girl who got me hemmed up back when I was working at Nexus?"

"Oh, yeah. That bullshit with the investigation and all that."

"Yeah. We got hired together."

"Fuck."

"Yeah. So while you on my head about a damn tuxedo, I'm dealing with her evil ass."

"You too pussy to handle working with a woman?"

My head pounded again. "That ain't got shit to do with it. I don't trust her ass."

"How she look?"

"How the fuck is *that* relevant?"

"I know you, that's how."

I sat there in angry silence. I hated how well my brother could read me.

"What I'm about to say doesn't change the fact that she's a horrible fucking person, but honestly? That girl is bad as *fuck*. Walked up in the Q&A like a fuckin' supermodel. And she was wearing these stockings, man. Black ones. Lace or some shit. They were—"

"I give it two weeks."

"What you mean?"

"Yall gon' be fuckin' by two weeks. Bet money."

I shut my mouth and thought about that. Obviously, I was attracted to her. I'm a man. But there was no clear path to sex, as I saw it. Not after the shit she pulled.

"How 'bout I change the subject?" I said. "Your bachelor party, nigga."

"What about it?"

"Savannah lettin' you off the leash, or not?"

"Aye, don't you worry about me and mine. Plan my shit and shut the fuck up."

Cussing each other out was our love language.

"Alright, I'll get with your fr—yo, do you even have any friends? I'ma need a list, cuz whoever they are, I ain't never met 'em."

"You ain't shit, you ain't never been shit, and you ain't never gon' be shit."

I laughed, painful as it was.

"Nah, for real, though. I'll send you the names. And as it relates to StarTech, I'ma tell you like this. I'm your big brother. I wouldn't steer you wrong. Don't ever let no woman fuck up your money, man."

"Said the nigga that's marrying his secretary."

"Former secretary, and yeah, cuz she been adding to my life since the day I met her. Ol' girl is stressin' you. That's different. Fuck all that shit in the past. Get your head in the game do your job."

"I hear you."

"Then maybe you'll finally become a millionaire like me."

"Fuck you."

"Yeah. And then after y'all fuck—"

"Ain't gonna happen."

"Nigga, five minutes ago you were waxing poetic about stockings. *Stockings*. Now, I love my lady with all my heart, but I couldn't tell you the first motherfucking thing about that shit."

"We like different things."

"Clearly."

I was just as surprised as he was. I can't say I ever paid attention before *she* showed up wearing them. But that wasn't about her, necessarily. It could have been anybody wearing them. It could have been my mama wearing them.

Actually, nah.

"How is Savannah?"

"'Bout to pop. I'm working my ass off to get shit straight so I can take leave when the baby comes."

"How much longer?"

"A month."

"Well, tell her I asked about her."

"I will. Alright then, Vic. Text me the minute you get your measurements. And I mean *before* you walk out the fucking shop. Then plan my shit. *Then* get your work done. Sound good?"

"Fuck off, T."

"Love you, too."

I chuckled as I ended the call. Me and that nigga had been through some shit.

All oldest brothers have the capacity to be assholes, but Taurus was on a different level. When our father died, he morphed into a hybrid big brother bully/authoritarian father that put me and Isaac, my youngest brother, through hell.

He meant well, I know, but the damage was done. It took a while, but we were all finally at a place where we could forgive and move on.

I checked the time and concluded I had a little over an hour before I had to meet the team over at StarTech. I got dressed and grabbed my shit so I could be downstairs by the time the car got here.

I was surprised I beat her to it. Sitting in the car all alone, I made use of my waiting time by locating a tailor a few blocks from the hotel. That would shut my brother up. Then I texted Isaac about this damn bachelor party. His ass wasn't helping, but I couldn't leave him out.

"Sir?"

I looked up at the driver. "It's Vic."

"Yes, sir. We're only a few blocks away, but New York traffic is always heavy in this area. If you wanna be there by nine, we need to leave in the next five minutes."

I nodded, then looked out the window for Electra. It wasn't like her to be late. I instinctively picked up my phone to call her before remembering I didn't have her number. We checked in separately, so I also didn't know where the hell her room was.

I could always go in and ask the front desk to call her, but that would make *me* late. I debated that for all of a minute before I decided to call them instead.

After a few minutes, the lady at the front desk came back on the line and told me there was no answer. At that point, there was nothing else for me to do but to go on to the office. We couldn't *both* be no-shows.

I was lowkey worried about her, which surprised me given how much I disliked her. I didn't wish ill on the woman. Not at all. I suppose I even felt a little responsible for her. She was on my team now, after all.

That shit still didn't feel right to me.

We pulled up in front of a skyscraper and I hopped out, poking my head back in to speak to my driver.

"What's your name?"

He turned to me. "Marcellus."

"Thank you, Marcellus. Enjoy your day, bruh."

"You, too. I'll see you back here after."

"Oh, alright then. 'Preciate it."

I made the short walk to the elevators, feeling worse and worse as I ascended to the twenty-third floor. I left her behind and I felt like shit about it, even after everything that happened.

So imagine my fucking surprise when I walked into the conference room and saw the Harpy sitting there next to Nora, laughing and having a good ass time.

"There he is!" That was some smiling white man I didn't know yet. "Victor, glad you made it."

It was only a few minutes after nine, but yeah, I was basically late.

"I apologize. Traffic was worse than anticipated." Embarrassed, I looked over at her. "I'm glad to see *you* made it. You didn't take the car."

She smiled slyly. "I had an errand to run before the meeting."

I took my seat, resigning myself to the fact that I would have to deal with her ass later on. I nodded at Nora and pulled out my iPad, my game face on.

We went through introductions and a few corny ass jokes before getting down to business. I locked in, determined to heed my brother's words.

But I couldn't help but sneak a few looks at her. All dressed up in gray. Face and hair perfect, as always. But she was my fucking enemy. I was trying to be nice with her for the money's sake, but fuck that. After what she pulled today, it was game on.

―――*ell*―――

> Measurements scheduled for today

Fuckin finally

> Party two weeks from Saturday

> Good. Yall fuck yet?

>> Ain't gonna happen. She pulled some petty shit today. I cant stand her ass

> So...three weeks?

>> STFU

>> Wifey cool with strippers?

> Yep

>> Savannah's a real one

> All day

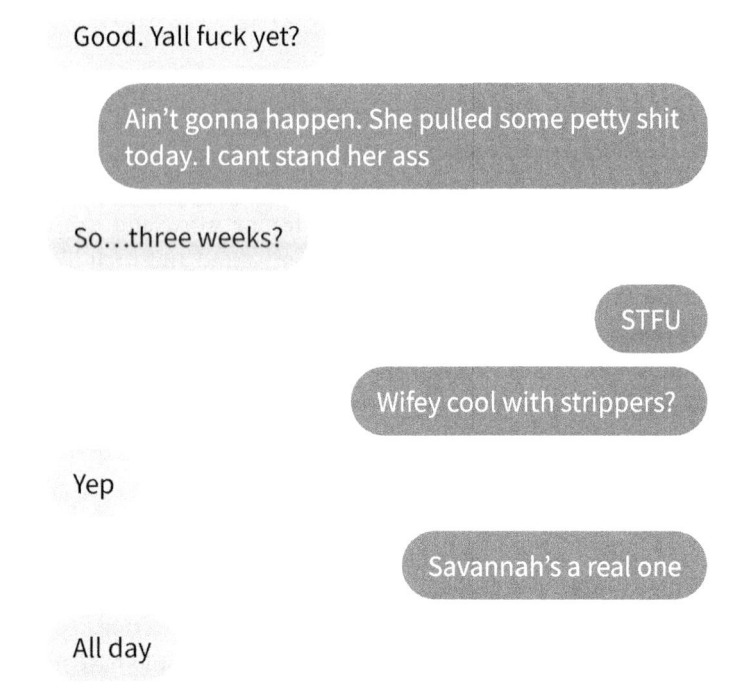

Good for his bitch ass.

My love life was...non-existent at this point. I was outside, and I wasn't struggling, but nobody was really doing it for me. I don't care how fine a woman is. If the chemistry isn't there, I can't rock with her past a date or two. The sex might keep me satisfied a little while longer, hoping I can carve out something real, but it never does.

I suppose I wanted what my brother had. At thirty-seven years old...yeah, it was time.

I had a date coming up once I got back home to Summerville. Jade seemed promising. Smart, accomplished, attractive. We met on an app and hit it off. But I'd been outside long enough to know not to get my hopes up.

I looked over at the woman next to me and felt the same way, but in business terms.

This shit wasn't gonna work.

"Are we gonna talk about that bullshit you pulled back there?"

Without looking up from her phone, she shrugged. "I had errands."

"And you didn't think to notify me so I wasn't sitting here waiting on you?"

She finally looked up. Her eyes burned with a fiery intensity that made me uncomfortable.

"Is that any different from you basically telling the client I'm an alcoholic?"

"That was a joke, Electra."

I shifted in my seat. The discomfort was growing more acute.

"Well, it wasn't funny, *Victor.*"

"So basically what I'm getting is that we're not capable of civility, even for the sake of the bag."

She sighed. "I just really, truly, do not like you."

"Same. I also don't trust you," I said. "That's not at issue. What's at issue is getting this project done."

Marcellus glanced at us in the rearview mirror.

She sighed. "Maybe we need to talk about the elephant in the room."

My eyebrows lifted at that. "I'm willing to hash it out."

"Oh, there's nothing to hash out. I was more so alluding to you apologizing to me."

I burst out laughing. The discomfort was gone. Now I was just pissed again. "Apologize. To you? Now *you* got jokes."

"You don't think I deserve an apology?"

"Hell, nah. It's the other way around, sweetheart."

It was her turn to laugh. More of a snicker, really. "You have a lot of nerve."

"And you have severe psychological problems if you think I'm apologizing to you for some shit I didn't do."

"Whatever, Victor. Fuck you."

"Oh! Fuck me? Look at little miss prim and proper cussing me out."

"Don't be condescending, asshole. I am not the one."

"Not the one. That's cute."

"Oh, now I'm cute?" She turned her body, facing me head on. "Listen, don't let the smooth taste fool you. You don't wanna spar with me. You have no idea who you're dealing with."

"On the contrary. I've experienced your treachery first hand, remember? Ain't nobody scared of you."

"You know, your whole tough guy act might be easier to believe if you weren't staring at my legs."

Fuck.

I didn't even realize.

My eyes shifted up to hers. "Ain't nobody staring. Your eyes never rest on something without you realizing?"

"Not like that."

"Like what?"

She smirked. "Like you're starving and you just walked into a buffet. Pervert."

I opened my mouth to speak, then closed it again, my eyes glancing up at Marcellus. The amusement on his face was irritating.

"Um, we're here," he said.

I wondered how long he'd been waiting for a chance to tell us that. I couldn't even remember stopping.

"Thanks, Marcellus." I grabbed my shit and opened the door. "See you tomorrow."

"Yes. Eight a.m."

I hurried my ass into the hotel and took a nap, then I ordered dinner before taking a quick shower and calling it a night. At nine-thirty.

This woman was stressing me out.

7

Electra

"Bloody Mary, please."

Victor declined a drink.

We were 1A and 1B again, and I needed a damn drink to get me through this.

Surprisingly, he left me alone. It would probably be more accurate to say he passed out and forgot where he was. I'd never seen a person sleep so hard on an airplane before.

He even slept through the landing. I was tempted to leave his ass right where he was, but something in me made me take pity on him.

I stared at his chiseled face and lamented my bad luck. In another life, this handsome, sexy, charming, accomplished man would be my type, and I'd be letting him wine and dine me and fold me up like a pretzel by now. Instead, we were like oil and water.

And it was all his fault.

I nudged him with my elbow.

Hard.

Bleary-eyed and nap-bewildered, he glared at me. I simply smiled and said, "We're here."

For some reason, he felt the need to walk with me to baggage claim. I sped up, using my high school track skills to ditch him, but to no avail.

Our eyes met across the crowded train car. He looked rough, like the sleep he'd gotten on the plane had been restless and fitful. Knowing him, he probably stayed up all night last night plotting my downfall.

I looked away, realizing I needed to keep my guard up. I couldn't give him another chance to bring me down. This was the first major account I'd gotten since I went out on my own. There was too much riding on this.

I was making my way toward baggage claim when Lance called me.

"Hey!"

"Hey, beautiful. You back?"

"Yeah, just landed a little while ago. How was your week?"

"Horrible without you."

"Oh, please," I laughed. "Mine was bad too, but for other reasons."

I glanced behind me, surprised Victor was right on my heels.

"Can I see you tonight?"

I paused, but not to think. There was nothing to ponder, really. Lance was a good stress reliever.

But I needed to strategize tonight.

"I'm kind of tired. And I can't do tomorrow. I have an event with the family that I have to get ready for. What about Monday?"

He sighed. "You're killing me, girl."

"I know. I'm terrible."

"You could never be terrible. Alright, then. Monday it is. I guess I don't have a choice."

"You don't. Text me the details."

"Sure thing, beautiful. Talk soon."

"Bye."

Behind me, I heard what can only be described as a derisive snort. I glanced back, knowing I'd see his handsome face twisted into some kind of bitter expression, but all I saw was smugness.

But why would he be smug?

He'd just heard me on the phone planning a date with another man. Not that I expected him to care, but still. I didn't like the way he was looking at me.

"What?" I finally demanded.

He eased past the man in front of him and picked up his pace next to me. "Was that one of the deserving people?"

"Why do you care?"

"Once again, I really don't. Just thought it was funny."

"You know what else is funny?"

"What's that, Electra?"

"This transparent attempt to get in my business and figure out if I'm dating somebody."

"Objectively speaking, you're an attractive woman. Of course you're dating."

"Well, thank—"

"Although I'm sure they turn tail and run once they find out how fucking evil you are."

Against my will, a laugh caught in my throat. I couldn't stand this man, but something about him amused me occasionally.

"I'm only mean to men who do me wrong."

"Still on that bullshit, I see."

"Whatever. I'm gonna leave you right here and go claim the baggage I actually *want*."

A smirk crossed his face. "Uh huh. See you Monday."

"Yes. And not by choice."

I left him where he stood, grateful to be out of his orbit for the first time in two days. Much as I hated to admit it, he was starting to...affect me.

One day later, I walked into Redeemer's Path Baptist Church. I was determined to be on my best behavior today, because today wasn't about me. It was about my big brother—by two years—and his triumph.

The thing about Emory...he was okay when it was just us. When our parents were around, it was a different story.

Being a Montrose isn't easy. So many goals. So many expectations for the children of a surgeon and a pharmacist. Emory had met them all. Graduated from seminary by twenty-five. Doctorate by twenty-nine. Married by thirty—to a dentist—and handing out grandkids by thirty-three. Then, senior pastor by thirty-six. He was the dream.

I'm the nightmare.

The Montrose family was tucked neatly in the front row, including Emory's wife Cassidy and my nieces Leah and Layla. I had no choice but to join them.

The girls gave me big smiles, and Cassidy waved. My parents just nodded at me. I was ten minutes late, after all.

I relaxed once I started reading the program. The ceremony was pretty regimented, which meant no free time for my beloved parents to get in my business. I would spend ten minutes at the reception after, then bow out, citing work obligations. It was partly true; I had an obligation to myself to mentally prepare for the battle ahead.

Victor Jackson wasn't going to catch me slipping again.

After making sure my ringer was off, I listened to a bunch of religious people I'd never met gush about the brother I'd known my entire life. I clapped when everyone else did, but I checked out right around the time the praise dancers took the stage.

My mind wandered aimlessly. I saw flashes of the Big Apple. The StarTech office. Nora. *Him*.

I hadn't wanted to admit it to myself, but the man actually looked better now than he did back then. Men are so fortunate that way.

I remembered how he lifted his arms to put his luggage in the overhead compartment. His shirts rode up, and I saw more than I wanted to see. I came to the conclusion that he had to be a regular in the gym. Abs like that require discipline. Good for him, I guess. I didn't want to see that, but good for him.

I also remembered the faint trail of black hair running down the center of those abs. I'd always appreciated that visual, in general, but not on him. It was actually disgusting. Sexy, but disgusting. I bet that was the exact path his beads of sweat took when he worked out...

They were clapping again.

I banged my hands together, grateful for the distraction from my wicked thoughts. In a church, of all places. *Shame* on me.

It's just...well, me and Ci were talking about this the other day: Men aren't fine like they used to be. Is it the water? The food? Climate change? Whatever the cause, it's a major problem. So when you see a man as relentlessly attractive as Victor Jackson, it makes an impression.

If only he wasn't a festering boil on the skin of humanity.

My brother was in the pulpit now. He was holding a plaque. I didn't even register Cassidy and the girls leaving the pew to join him up there. Weird.

I smiled at the scene. Em could win all the awards the church could give him and be hoisted on the shoulders of his flock and paraded around Summerville, but he'd always be my goofy brother.

After, we took pictures. I deftly avoided placing myself in my parents' line of fire, sticking close to the girls, pretending I was helping out. That was easy.

The reception was the real challenge.

As *soon* as I picked up a plate, my mother appeared next to me. It was a jump scare.

"Are you avoiding me?"

I managed to fend off an eyeroll, but the sigh rushed out before I could stop it.

"What?" she demanded. "You think I didn't notice?"

"I wasn't. I just...it's Em's night. I figured y'all would wanna direct your attention to him."

"Mm hm. Nice try. What happened in New York?"

The woman was five feet three inches of perfection. Head to toe, she put me to shame. But one thing I'd learned early that seemed to be lost on her was the fact that the people closest to you can always see through the facade. And what I saw and heard from my mother was fear. Fear that someone would find a flaw.

"New York was fine. I'm on a major account." I turned around to spoon a helping of green beans onto my plate. "Everything's fine."

"Are you getting paid?"

I clenched my jaw a few times. "Yes. I'm getting paid."

"So is this...will it be enough for you to support yourself?"

I added a piece of salmon. "Yes, Mama."

"Well, that's wonderful, then. Your daddy will be happy to hear that."

"I haven't asked y'all for anything in a while."

"But you must be dipping into your savings by now. It's just a matter of time, I think."

Emory walked up just then, which was the best thing for all involved.

"Congratulations!" I said to him. "I'm proud of you."

"Thank you." He kissed my cheek, then wrapped an arm around our mother. "You gonna eat, Ma?"

"After I get your sister to be honest with me."

She put on that pout I always hated because it worked so well. Sure enough, Em switched allegiances. It felt like I could see into his brain.

"What happened?" he asked defensively.

"She says she has a new job, but—"

"It's a new account, and it's a major one."

Em frowned. "You said that last time."

"Hey, how about this? We all stop worrying about me and focus on this joyous occasion. Yes?"

The two of them looked at each other, sharing something only the two of them understood, likely about what a loser I am compared to him.

Just then, my father came into view. That was my cue to go. Couldn't let the three of them clique up. I'd gotten so distracted by the food offerings I forgot about my exit strategy.

I managed to get out of there five minutes later after quick hugs and kisses. I had to balance my plate on my lap while I drove home to my apartment, but that salmon was well worth it.

I ate in front of the television like I normally do, content with my surroundings. I'd have a house one day, but this would do for now. So would solitude.

I always seemed to feel content in the moment, but maybe that was the problem. Every moment eventually adds up to forever. I didn't want to be sitting here alone for the rest of my life, looking good on the outside but just barely keeping it all together. I *was* blowing through my savings. I *had* been living and dying by every little account I could land, hoping to turn it into something that would secure my future. This StarTech project was it. It was my last hope.

Not that my mother was right.

I'd never admit to that.

8

VIC

STARTECH SET US UP in a corner office on the sixth floor of their Summerville building. Me, Nora, and the she wolf. I beat her in today, which I did on purpose, but I knew she and her stockings would be darkening the doorway soon enough.

I beat Nora, too, so I had a little time to set myself up and chill with a cup of coffee before I had to be social. Unlike many people, I don't hate Mondays. Every Monday is a new opportunity to make money, as far as I'm concerned. I'm not a big fan of being social in the office, though.

Maybe I just didn't like people all that much.

"Good morning!" Nora cheered as she breezed into the room. "Getting the worm, huh?"

"Yes, ma'am."

It was a figure of speech, but I regretted it immediately. Women can be sensitive about their ages. As good as Nora looked, she was obviously older, and I didn't want her feeling like I'd auntied her.

But her face told me it was just fine. She didn't even blink. She simply picked a desk and set up, humming and erecting pictures like she was in this for the long haul.

"How was your weekend?" I said. Small talk was a necessary evil.

"It was fine. I got here yesterday. I went to that brunch place, Yellow. It was amazing!"

She and her husband were in a rental here for the duration of the project, courtesy of StarTech.

"Yeah, we got some spots out here," I agreed. "If you ever need a guide, I'm here. As long as your husband's okay with that."

"Oh, hush," she laughed and pointed a finger at me. "You're trouble."

I nodded. "I've been told."

"I bet. If I was twenty years younger…"

"Morning, Nora!"

Her.

I turned in my chair, putting my attention on my laptop screen. I'd caught a glimpse of her, though, and it was a pleasant one. A torturous one.

It was almost annoying how good she looked.

She had a date tonight, too. I remembered that from her conversation in the airport. That must have been why she looked so good. And smelled so good.

Good luck to him, whoever he was.

"Look at you!" Nora said in that voice women use when they're gassing each other up. "Who is that?"

"Just Ralph Lauren."

"I love it."

"Thank you."

It was strange hearing genuine cheer in her voice. I turned my head toward them, regretting it immediately when I saw Electra standing at Nora's desk, giving me a bird's eye view of the back of her body.

Green dress. Modest length, but the fit was of the body-skimming variety, making her tempting curves apparent. My eyes went straight to the curve of her waist, and before I could stop them, they fell south, settling on her round, perky ass. Why didn't I notice that before? No time to wonder, because my eyes seemed to be moving independently of my brain. Down they traveled until they landed on her legs, which were covered, again, in black stockings. This time, the pattern was argyle, and I followed those diamonds up and down, mesmerized until I realized Nora was watching me.

I ain't no punk, but I also didn't want my attention to detail to be mistaken for interest, so I averted my eyes immediately, which probably only served to make me look guilty.

"Alright, since we're all here," I said pointedly, "we might as well go ahead and divvy up the tasks."

Electra turned toward me. "I already laid out a plan. I can email it to you if you like."

"I think it would make more sense for us to work on the plan together."

She crossed her arms. "But I already have one."

"And I might not like it."

"That's sounds like a *you* problem."

"Seeing as how we're on the same team, I would argue it's an *us* problem."

I glanced over at Nora, noting the confused look on her face.

We were already fucking this up.

"How about this?" I put on my best, most congenial voice. "I'll look at your list and revise it with my input, then we'll meet in the middle."

It took her way too long to agree to my very reasonable suggestion, and even when she agreed, it was begrudgingly, with a weak nod and eye roll.

Ignoring that bullshit, I checked my inbox and there it was.

Maleficent's email.

> *Greetings.*
>
> *While you were snoring on the plane, I was being productive in preparation for the start of our project. As such, I put together a list of tasks, and I would appreciate it if you looked at it ASAP. There's a lot to do and time is finite.*

As I read her list, I wasn't surprised to find that she hadn't missed a single detail. I honestly had no notes, and that pissed me off, because it was bad enough that she already thought she was perfect. The fact that her work fit the bill really got under my skin.

I sat there for several minutes trying to come up with some feedback, but I realized I was wasting time and energy. It's not like I *wanted* to fail on this project. If her grand plan was to one-up me and do everything ten minutes before I did, she could have that shit. I didn't have a damn thing to prove.

> *Greetings.*
> *This seems adequate.*

> *I suggest we divide the gap analysis into two different sectors; performance and product. I'll focus on the former. You can take the latter. Also, please CC Nora on all communications as I've done here. Thanks.*

It seemed like only a full minute passed before she was sauntering toward my desk with a frown sitting on her face. I say sauntered because, well, her walk was irritatingly sensual. I had to actively work against my natural instinct, which was yet another thing about her that pissed me off.

More specifically, her hips swayed from left to right. A lot. And her shapely legs bowed ever so slightly, which was yet another curve on her that I couldn't manage to ignore. Even the click of her high heels on the wood floor made me think of things I had no business imagining. Like those legs wrapped around my waist.

But that's the thing about fantasies. They're temporal, and our awareness of this fact keeps us from going too deep.

A fantasy was all it would ever be with Evilena.

"Need something?" I said as she came to a stop right in front of me.

"You just *had* to find something to criticize."

I smiled. "Suggestions are only criticisms if you're the kind of person who takes everything personally."

Her nostrils flared. "What makes you think I should take product? On what did you base that decision?"

"I guess the same thing you based your decision on when you took it upon yourself to make the list on your own."

"Okay, so...is there an issue you two need to resolve?"

Me and Electra shared a glance, then looked away quickly. I hadn't even realized Nora had crept up on us.

"What do you mean?" I said, stalling for time.

Nora wasn't with the bullshit, I could tell. Older women never are. She shot me a look that wasn't unlike one my mother would give me when I was trying to finesse my way out of something.

"I sense tension," she finally said. "It's okay, there's always tension on a team. I just think we'll be more productive if we hash it out and move on. Whatever it is."

Funny. Those were the same words I'd said to Electra, and she refused. Which signaled to me that *she* was the problem, not me.

"I'm good," I said, and that was the truth. "Honestly, yeah, there's tension, but it won't stop me from doing my job."

Through gritted teeth, Electra said, "Same here. Victor, I think your suggestion was a good one. Let's go with that."

"Glad you agree."

With Nora behind her, Electra apparently felt free to pull a face that I could only read as utter contempt. After, she rolled her eyes, finally turning on her heels to walk away from me.

I sat there dumbstruck. Not because of her little tantrum. That shit didn't faze me. My problem was that I had just realized my brother was right.

Maybe not about the timeline. That was still debatable. But it was very clear to me in that moment that I wanted her. And since I'm one of God's favorites, and tend to get what I want, it only meant one thing.

The countdown was on.

9

Electra

"You like that?"

How do you answer that question during sex with an attractive man who just isn't doing it for you? Men have egos, after all. Although to be fair, I *did* like it, in that I appreciated what he was doing. It just wasn't getting me any closer to where I needed to be. And that was strange, because Lance was usually pretty reliable.

"Yes," I moaned from underneath him. Lance loved missionary, which suited me just fine. Less to do. But I wasn't a pillow princess. Far from it. I can get loose when the chemistry is there.

"You feel so good," he groaned in my ear. Pumping away. Nice strokes. Consistent rhythm. Slightly above average length and girth. I stared up at his face, dark brown, smooth, and impossibly symmetrical, and felt frustrated. Lance had all the ingredients, but I just wasn't getting there tonight.

Maybe it was my mental state. I just couldn't seem to focus. Between the project, the tension, and Victor…I probably wasn't gonna have another orgasm until my next job.

"What's wrong?"

I blinked, only realizing just then that he'd stopped.

"I'm sorry." I grabbed his face. "Too much on my mind. Keep going."

His face fell. That pesky ego thing. I leaned up to kiss him, but he pulled away. I watched as he pulled out, then sat up to look down at me.

"You're leaving?"

"Nah, just trying something else."

The last thing I said before his head was between my legs was, "Oh." That led to, "Ohhhhhhhhhh," and then my fingers were threaded in his hair. His shoulder-length locs brushed against my thighs as I closed my eyes and went limp. This would work. It always did.

But five minutes later, a seed of doubt sprouted in my mind. Despite Lance's exceptional tongue work and my intense arousal, nothing was happening.

What is wrong with me?

We met at an art gallery. Ciara dragged me along that night. I had a cold and would have rather been on my couch with a steaming hot bowl of chicken soup. But Lance...he made it worth it. Some of his paintings were on display, which he proudly announced to us as soon as we entered the gallery.

We'd been sleeping together ever since.

Five minutes turned to ten, which turned to long enough for me to know it wasn't happening for me tonight.

"Lance." He kept eating, so I nudged his head. "Lance. It's okay. You can stop."

His head popped up. "Seriously, what's wrong?"

I sat up and pulled the sheet over me. "I just started this new job. It's stressful. I don't know. My mind is all over the place."

"Anything I can do?"

He didn't mean it. It's just one of those things you say to the person you're in a situation with. So I shook my head and leaned in to kiss him, hoping that would be signal enough to get him out of here.

After he left, I took a quick shower, slathered myself in lotion and body oil, then curled up in my bed.

The dissatisfaction was like a splinter, nagging and stinging me, but it was in too deep for me to get any relief.

I dialed up Ci and hoped she'd have an answer for me.

"Hey. You busy?"

"Headed to the movies. What's wrong?"

"Lance was just here."

"Ooh, okay. And you ain't pass out afterwards?"

I laughed at her foolishness. "That was one time. And no. Definitely not. I couldn't...get there."

"That's not good. Did his dick get smaller?"

"No, stupid." I blew out a sigh. It was time to come clean, with myself as much as her. "It wasn't him at all. You know Lance is fine, and he knows what he's doing. It was me."

"Did you need lube?"

"Everything was working the way it was supposed to, Ci. I think it's mental."

"Yeah, stress will do it. Is it work?"

"Gotta be. Working with *him*...I mean, it has to be that, right? Being around him isn't good for me. I'm on edge. I have to keep an eye on my computer at all times. We bickered all day today, nothing really got done, and we were super petty with each other in front of the client."

I was still pissed about that. And it wasn't just him. I played an equal part. We were in the discovery phase, which is vital. It sets the tone for the entire project. Yet we still found time to act like fools.

"So just give him five fingers to the face and keep it pushing," she said.

"Don't think I haven't thought about it. But for real, I need a real solution."

"Confront him. Once and for all. This is business. And I know you know how to handle yourself at work, so I can't figure out why you're being all lightweight with him."

"You know what? You're right."

"As always."

"I'm gonna go in tomorrow and be the bad bitch I am. Thank you for reminding me."

It was so simple. I'd let him get me off my square, but no more.

I was going to go in there and settle this, and then we were going to be a real team.

I didn't have to like him to work with him.

10

VIC

Electra stomped in on Tuesday morning with her Starbucks cup in her hand and a pinched look on her face.

Poor baby. Whoever she had a date with obviously didn't do his job last night.

If she'd gone out with me, she wouldn't have that problem. I'd have her limping in here with a smile on her face and purple suck marks on her ass.

I brushed that out of my mind.

She wore black slacks, and that was for the best. No gawking at her legs today. I could focus.

"I need to talk to you."

I looked around for Nora. "Me?"

She rolled her eyes. "Yes. You."

I saved the report I was working on and locked my computer. "What's up?"

She took a long sip of her drink, then set it on her desk.

"I don't like our work environment. I think it's unnecessarily tense and hostile."

"Okay..."

"As such, I thought it was best to clear the air."

I bit back the urge to remind her I wanted to do this days ago.

I nodded at her to continue.

"What happened at Nexus was unfortunate. We both blamed each other, and it seems we're both still holding onto those grudges."

I nodded again.

"I'm willing to let my grudge go if you tell me why you did it."

My face balled up until it was a mirror image of hers. "Are you serious?"

"Yes. Tell the truth. For once. It would be very helpful."

"It's not the fucking truth, Electra. I had no part in any of that shit. To this day, I don't know how they got access to my computer. The logical conclusion I drew was that it was you. So how about *you* tell the truth? Admit what you did. It would be helpful," I mocked.

"The investigation didn't find any wrongdoing on my part."

"And it didn't find any on mine either, so what the fuck are we talking about?"

She took a deep breath, crossing her arms in front of her. "Why on earth would you think I would do that?"

"To get ahead? To separate yourself from me? To sabotage me?"

She shook her head.

"Why would you think *I* would do it?"

"Honestly? I think you were threatened by me. A powerful black woman with a better background and more accomplishments. People are threatened by perfection."

Laughter burst out of me. "Perfection?"

"I meant *perceived* perfection."

"And you still ain't in the ballpark, sweetheart."

"Don't call me sweetheart."

I stared at her. "Get over yourself, Electra. You aren't perfect. I don't *perceive* you as perfect. Never have. And your alleged power and background and whatever else has nothing to do with why I didn't like you back then, or why I don't care for you now."

"Then what is it?"

"You came through the door with your fucking nose in the air. Talking about your pedigree and your Ivy League degrees. When I told you what schools I went to, you acted like I said I was a drug dealer."

"And I turned you down for a date."

I spread my hands. "That was probably the *least* offensive thing you did. You were one of several women I asked out. Win some, lose some." I chuckled. "I mean, look at me. I wasn't trippin' off you."

"Wow. Okay. Well, as far as the other things, I can maybe see how..." she trailed off, staring down at the floor. "*Maybe* I was a little insufferable back then."

I nodded.

"I probably felt like I had something to prove. There's some deeper stuff there that...anyway," she rushed out. "That was my thinking."

"Is that an apology?"

"Not at all. It's me telling you I don't wanna spend the next few weeks at each other's throats, especially in front of Nora. We called a truce before, but it wasn't built on a solid foundation."

"Because you were still being petty."

"Because we were *both* still being hostile to each other."

I shrugged. "It's whatever. I'm trying to get this money. That's all. Either you're on board or you're not."

"I am."

"Good. Check your email. They sent us the access codes for the files and databases."

Without so much as a blink of acknowledgment, she seated herself at her desk and put me on ignore. All I could think about was whether or not she could be trusted this time around.

———

So Jade turned out to be a dub.

Mind you, the woman was pretty as hell. Smart. A junior executive at a marketing firm. Funny, too, and the conversation was pretty good.

But I didn't feel a spark.

I felt bad about it, too, because I pursued her pretty hard once I swiped right on her on Paired. On paper, she was exactly what I was looking for.

We were only five minutes into dinner when I knew this wasn't going anywhere.

As we talked over sushi and sake, and she was telling me a hilarious story about her firm getting fired by Google, I was having an internal debate about whether I was toxic or not.

Conventional male wisdom says we want women who give us peace. We want women who are nice. Who are sweet. And she was all of those things, so far. But did *I* really want that? It was a question that needed an answer because I was bored out of my fucking mind.

The only logical conclusion I could draw was that *I* must be toxic. Maybe there was some internal wound that hadn't healed yet. Mommy issues? Perhaps.

That said, the fact that I was self aware enough to even wonder about this made me feel good, because I didn't know any men who asked themselves hard questions. Every man I know operates from the base assumption that ain't shit wrong with us.

So, yeah.

I gave myself a mental pat on the back for being ahead of the curve. Probably just an inch or two ahead, but it was something.

I also gave myself credit a short while later when I walked her to her front door and didn't go in. I had a green light, too, but I told her I had an early day tomorrow. I did kiss her, but I didn't feel a thing. Felt like someone injected lidocaine into my lips.

She smiled when I told her I'd call her. I drove away from her condo with every intention to do just that. But by the time I pulled into my driveway, I knew it would be pointless to call her with anything other than an apology for wasting her time.

11

Electra

Still no orgasm.

I worked my ass off last night trying to make it happen, too. My rose failed me. My fingers disappointed me. Even Old Faithful, my trusty oscillating shower head, let me down.

To say I was frustrated would be the ultimate understatement.

And it was all Victor's fault. I was convinced of it, now. Because he was all I could think about while I pleasured myself. Not his face. Not his body. Nothing that would further my pleasure. I was stuck on everything he'd done to me, and the fact that I was trapped on this project with him. Not exactly an aphrodisiac.

Something had to give.

Right now, he was at his desk, typing something and leaving me the hell alone. I was thankful for that, at least. Nora was off doing StarTech stuff, and I was preparing to conduct stakeholder interviews.

A short blonde man walked in, knocking on the door as he passed through it.

"I'm here to see someone named Electra."

I gave him a smile. "That's me. Ellis, is it?"

He nodded.

"Thanks for meeting with me."

"Didn't have much of a choice."

I smiled again, but it was colder this time. "Well anyway, glad you could make it. Please, have a seat."

While he settled onto the chair I'd set up opposite mine, I looked behind me to glare at Victor's back. I don't know why. There was no reason. It just felt right.

I turned back to Ellis. "I just have a few questions, and then I'll let you get back to your work. First, I want to ask you about your current workflows. Walk me through a typical software development cycle."

Ellis sat back and looked at me with curiosity. "Is that your area?"

"I'm sorry?"

"Are you even *in* tech?"

I blinked a few times as I made sense of his question. "I'm a consultant," I finally answered.

"Right, but is tech your area?"

"Why do you ask?"

He chuckled. "It just seems like such a basic question."

Behind me, the typing sounds stopped, leaving the room eerily silent.

I took a deep breath and let *first of all, bitch* play out in my head rather than come out of my mouth. "The questions I'm asking you were selected for a reason. Are you able to answer?"

Ellis Healey, regular staff front end developer, shrugged with an arrogance typically reserved for titans of industry.

"I mean, yeah, I can answer, but it might make more sense for you to..." he trailed off, his eyes rising to focus on something above my head. An object dragged across the floor, making an odd sound as it moved closer to me. I was just about to turn around when Victor came into view on my right side. The chair he held came to a stop just before he planted himself in it.

Ellis looked at me, then at Victor, and waited. I waited, too, wondering what he would say, but he didn't say a word. His glare—aimed directly at Ellis—seemed to say more than enough.

Ellis cleared his throat. "Um, so our software development process usually begins with requirements gathering. That's when we collaborate with stakeholders to define project objectives and scope. Once that's done, our developers move on to design, coding, testing, and deployment. Maintenance comes last."

I smiled. "Thank you. See, that wasn't so hard, was it?"

Victor snickered.

"In your experience," I continued, "what are some common challenges or bottlenecks your team encounters during this process?"

"Mostly communication and collaboration between our development, testing, and operations teams. We always have delays because of miscommunication or issues with version control. Also, trying to get our development environments to mirror production environments can be a big hurdle."

I nodded along, writing bullet points on my tablet. The questions and answers continued to flow, and Victor eventually returned to his desk, leaving his chair behind. Ellis kept glancing at it, which amused me to no end. Even that man's empty seat was a threat.

Something about that was...well, I was glad he was on my team.

I didn't have any problems after that. After seven more employee interviews, I put a pin in that part of the project and broke for lunch. I grabbed my snacks out of my tote and set them on the conference table. StarTech had already stocked it with goodies, but it was all processed food, and I was making an attempt to eat healthier.

I went off in search of napkins. I must have been wandering aimlessly, because a tall black man with a cleft chin walked up to me to ask, "Are you lost?"

I smiled up at all six feet five of him. At least. "I am, actually. Do I look lost?"

"You look like you're in a daze. Are you new here?"

"I'm a consultant. And yes, I'm new."

He stuck out his hand. "I'm Qadir. Head of security."

"Oh!" I gave him a firm shake. "I'm Electra. Was this little meeting an accident, or were you watching me?"

He chuckled. "I had no idea who you were, but I must admit, I was definitely watching you."

I broke the stare after that, because it wasn't the least bit subtle, and I wasn't here for that. "Well, I'm wandering around because I'm looking for napkins. Can you point me to the break room?"

"I can do that for you, Ms. Electra."

I followed him down a hallway to a large room on the left. We caught stares, but I ignored that. The downside of being the new kid on the block.

Qadir waited while I gathered the napkins from the counter. Once I made my way back to the door, he smiled again.

"Can you find your way back, or do you need an escort?"

"I think I can find it. Thank you."

"Yes, ma'am."

He sauntered off, leaving me wondering if our little interaction was by chance. After what happened at Nexus, I admit to being a little paranoid about companies' perceptions of me. Word travels fast in my industry, and labels are hard to remove.

Back in our little makeshift office, both Nora and Victor were hard at work. I made my way to the table only to find there was something missing.

I stared at my grapes, then at Victor. "Why did you take my snack?"

He frowned. "What snack?"

"I left these grapes and a bag of chocolate covered almonds on the table."

"Oh, yeah, I ate the almonds. They were sitting there where the snacks have been for the last few days, so..."

"But that wasn't for everybody," I said, my voice rising. "Those were mine. I was coming right back for them. I just went to get napkins!"

"My bad, Electra. I didn't realize. I'll buy you some more."

I narrowed my eyes as I regarded him. He seemed sincere. His face registered concern. But I put nothing past him.

"That's not the point," I muttered. "I had my mouth all fixed to eat those damn almonds. Am I gonna have to start writing my name on all my food?"

"Why'd you ask me and not Nora?"

I rolled my eyes. "I knew she didn't do it."

"So I'm a thief?"

"Clearly."

I locked eyes with Nora. I forgot she was here, and that she was listening to this petty argument.

"It's fine," I muttered. "Next time, ask."

His jaw clenched. "Sure thing, Electra."

Yeah, we were doing a bang-up job at this teamwork thing.

But, like...who eats somebody else's food? Okay, yes, the table was full of snacks. But the almonds and grapes were new! Logic should have dictated that...actually, I doubted that man had a logical thought in his brain. All he knew was impulse, as evidenced by his behavior twelve years ago.

I was so wrong. I couldn't work with him. I couldn't be cordial and treat him like a teammate.

But what other choice did I have?

12

Vic

I DIDN'T REALLY THINK this through.

The logistics of making it happen seemed simple when I was at the Nature's Fruit warehouse yesterday, but now that I was trudging across the parking deck carrying it, I was having second thoughts.

By the time I reached the office, I was sweating buckets under my suit. But I persevered, because I was on a mission.

"Morning, Ms. Nora! Don't you look lovely today?"

She turned in her chair and beamed. "Thank you, sugar." She eyed me curiously. "What's all that?"

"Just replacing the snacks I stole."

I dropped the ten-pound box onto Electra's desk, ignoring Nora's amused stare as I took great care to arrange her things around it. She struck me as a neat freak, so far be it for me to disturb that.

Once everything was back in its place, I gave Nora a nod and settled in at my workstation. Electra had finished her interviews, so I had a full day of qualitative coding ahead of me.

The familiar click of her heels brought a smile to my face.

"Good morning, Nora!"

"Morning, dear."

She stopped. "Did I get a delivery? What is this?"

I turned around just in time to see Nora look over at me and shake her head. I could tell she was both tickled and perplexed by my antics. Truth be told, I didn't even fully understand the shit I was doing. Deep down, I suppose I wanted to antagonize Electra a little bit. That was obvious. But at this moment, I realized I also wanted to make her laugh. Even a smile would do.

But there was none of that.

She stared at the box, confused and bewildered.

"Open it," I said. "I delivered it special just for you."

She cut her eyes at me, then flipped the top of the box open. She stared for a few seconds before saying, "Really, Victor?"

I shrugged. "I felt bad about eating your snacks, so I made sure to replace them. With a little extra."

"A *little*?" She wrapped her arms around the box and attempted to lift it. No dice. "This box weighs more than I do."

"Hyperbole," I said. "Would you like me to help you move it?"

She glanced at Nora, who quickly looked away and tried to pretend she was busy working. She wanted no parts of this. Then again, she was watching and listening to it like it was a one-act play we'd written especially for her.

"Please get this off my desk," Electra said, her tone sharp. "Some of us have work to do."

I stood and walked over to her. "Sure. I'll help you out. I don't mind at all."

"No, this isn't help. You did this to be petty."

"I did this because I felt bad about accidentally eating your snack. Had I known—"

"Just move it," she snapped.

"Is that necessary?"

In a whisper, she said, "You know she's hearing all of this. Grow up."

When she put it that way...

Sometimes I forgot Nora was the client. She was so friendly and auntie-esque. But Cersei Lannister was right. I needed that wakeup call.

Going forward, I would only piss her off when Nora wasn't here to witness it.

I raised my arms to grab the box. Since she didn't bother to move out of the way, I accidentally grazed her with my right hand. My brain seemed to be working slower than my eyes. I knew where I'd touched her, but the sensation was delayed.

I'd grazed her breast.

She sucked in a breath, and when my eyes met hers, I saw her shudder.

"I am *so* sorry," I said. "Truly, sincerely, I apologize. I didn't mean to—"

"I know. It was an accident." She brushed her hair back, tucking it behind her ear. "Just move the box, please."

Done with the games, and feeling terrible, I did as she asked, transferring the box to the floor next to her desk.

"Let me know when you leave and I'll take it out to your car."

She nodded.

"Listen, it was petty. I'm an asshole sometimes. I apologize."

She didn't say a word, but the tension in her body told me she had plenty to say. She seemed stuck, so I moved a little closer. "You okay? I understand if you're upset."

Still, nothing.

I was confused until my gaze dropped a few inches. My lips parted as the realization hit me.

The heather grey dress she wore was too thin to hide the evidence. Her nipples poked indecently, straining against the fabric while I stared and prayed my dick wouldn't get hard.

She cleared her throat. "Check your email," was all she said as she turned swiftly, cutting off my view.

I trudged back to my desk with my mind racing. I opened that email, read it, and didn't retain shit. All I could think about was what I'd just seen, and whether there were other things happening that I didn't see.

Because usually…nah.

Don't do it.

Don't fucking do it.

If I let myself think about it, I wouldn't get shit done today.

So with every ounce of willpower, I cleared my mind and focused on something other than Electra.

But one thing was for sure.

The countdown clock had just sped up.

13

Electra

I couldn't focus.

On work, anyway.

All I'd been able to think about for the past few days was getting back at Victor Jackson.

Between interviews, surveys, and emails, I had no time to formulate a plan, much less a *good* plan, which is what I'd need to drive the point home, once and for all, that I was not the one.

I was still pissed about that little stunt he pulled with the almonds. He did end up loading them into my trunk that day, and I guess it wasn't the worst thing in the world to have my favorite snack conveniently stockpiled in an easily accessible place, but it was the *principle,* dammit.

Having said that, it wasn't just the almonds.

I was still embarrassed by the other thing that happened that day. I knew it was an accident, and I knew he felt horrible about it. That much was clear. No, I was humiliated by my body's betrayal. My nipples had never been that hard before. And I mean *ever*. I was stunned. Too stunned to move out of his line of sight.

Then it got worse.

When I saw him staring, the magnitude of the moment, the weight of it landed right between my legs.

I cringed every time I thought about how wet I got.

He and Nora had just gone to lunch together, giggling and sniggling like two teenagers. Nora would never admit it, but that woman had a crush on him. She'd never act on it, of course, but anyone could see it. Always laughing at his lame jokes. Complimenting him. Batting her eyelashes. It was quite irritating, and I say that as someone who had come to really like her.

I activated sleep mode on my laptop. Couldn't give anyone a chance to do something shady. Looking around the quiet office, I decided to take the opportunity to get inspired by walking over to Victor's desk to snoop.

No pictures. That wasn't surprising. Granted, I didn't have any either, but still. Noted.

Did he have family? Friends? I didn't care, but I was curious. I wondered who raised him. Your family of origin says a lot about you and who you'll become.

A brief flash of self-awareness reminded me that that was true for me as well, so I moved on.

A smile crossed my lips as I stared down at his closed notebook. More specifically, at the pen sitting on top.

A black and gold Visconti. I was impressed he'd even heard of them, much less owned one. Emory and I got one for my father for his last birthday.

It was lame and toothless, but it was all I had in my arsenal at this point. I picked up the pen and buried it in his desk drawer between stacks of paper.

I was at home in my bed eating a pint of Haagen Daas when my father called. I would have screened, but not after running out of the anniversary reception last week.

"Hey, Daddy. I was just thinking about you."

My father's snort came through loud and clear, as did its meaning.

"If you were thinkin' bout me, why didn't you call?"

Lord knows I loved this loud, country man, but my goodness. It could never just be a simple call or visit. There always had to be some guilt involved.

"I've been swamped with work," I finally answered. "How are you? How are things at the hospital?"

"Same as it ever was. Almost lost a patient yesterday, but God had other plans."

"Wow. I'm glad they pulled through."

"Mm hm."

Silence ensued. Dr. Montrose never used any more words than he had to. Or felt like.

"Excited about your birthday?"

"Mm hm. I guess. You comin'?"

"Of course. Mama didn't tell me what you want, though. Any ideas?"

"Just to see your pretty face."

I smiled at that.

"Uhh, also, just as an aside, I have a lead for you."

"A lead on what?"

"A job."

I set my dulce de leche on my nightstand. "I have a job, Daddy."

"Yeahhhhh, but..." he trailed off, going silent once again. But we both knew what he left unsaid.

"I worry about you," he finally said. "I know you're sticking with this thing, but it might be time to pivot. You've been at it long enough.

I pinched the bridge of my nose. "This is actually a pretty big account for me. It means things are looking up."

"If it goes well," he said.

"Right. Which I'm sure it will."

He sighed. "So do you want the lead or not?"

"What's the company?"

"Well, it's a position with First Bank. Pays well. Lots of room for advancement."

"Consulting?"

"No, it's a general manager position."

"But I don't work in banking, Daddy."

"You have an MBA from Ross. They'll hire you, Lex. I know the man. It's a sure thing."

I had an MBA from Ross because that's where they told me to go, not because it meant anything to me.

"Text me his info."

At this point, why not? I was losing hope, and my parents' constant questions and lack of faith in me wasn't helping. Because they very well may have been right.

The thought of it plagued me for the rest of the night. In fact, I was still thinking about it when Lance got here.

And despite his valiant efforts, there was no grand finale. There wasn't even a weak stumble across the finish line. There was nothing.

I did discover that thinking about the other day with Victor got me going, but that just made the lack of a climax even more frustrating.

After Lance left, I came to a disturbing conclusion.

There was a distinct possibility that Victor might be the solution to this problem.

14

Vic

In the platinum suite of the Regal Royale, Summerville's newest hotel, fifteen of us gathered to celebrate my brother's entree into marriage. Again.

The gang was all here, although I have to admit, I didn't know who half the gang was. Taurus didn't have a lot of friends—any friends, really—but that nigga had acquaintances out the ass.

The liquor was flowing, the cigars were burning, and he was in a chipper mood. Isaac wasn't much help with this whole bachelor party thing, but it was all good. I had it handled.

I know how to throw a party.

"Gentlemen," I addressed the crowd. "It's almost ten o'clock."

"What happens at ten?" Taurus asked.

"At ten, we toast. At ten-fifteen, the entertainment arrives."

That got them all smiling.

It's juvenile, I guess, but it's tradition. And since Savannah was down, I reached out to Brandy, a stripper I dated back in the day, and had her send some of her friends.

"Raise them glasses real quick." I waited for the glasses to rise and the smoke to clear. "Aight, so, as the best man—"

"One of," Isaac interrupted.

"One of," I repeated. "As *one of* the best men, and one of Taurus' best friends, and one of Taurus' only friends," I said to laughter, "I wanna congratulate him on bagging another bad bitch. I don't know how this ornery nigga does it, but here we are."

He laughed and nodded at that.

"But seriously, Savannah's a good woman. She's perfect for you. I really haven't seen anything like it. Not in a long time. Yall got that old-school shit. Yall *fit*, know what I mean?"

He nodded.

"Strip all the other shit away, and that's what it comes down to. Do y'all give each other what you need? I've seen it. Yall do. So congratulations, T. I'm happy for you, and I wish you a lifetime of nothing but happiness."

"Cheers!"

We drank to that as Isaac stood to his feet.

"Yeah, I gotta agree with Vic. I ain't never seen you this happy, man. Or this nice."

We laughed again.

"Any woman that can turn my brother from beast to man is alright in my book. So, cheers, man. I love you and I'm happy for you."

We drank to that, then Ricardo, who was playing DJ tonight, turned the music back on.

Taurus made his way over to me. His smile still lowkey didn't sit well with me these days. I just wasn't used to it.

"I appreciate you, man. You did good."

I shrugged. "It's what I do."

I was dapping him up when I heard a knock at the door.

"They're here," I said to him. "You sure wifey is cool?"

"Wifey is cool. She would have been here with me if she wasn't pregnant."

I laughed and made my way to the door, yelling out, "Ayo! This ain't finna be like *The Best Man*. My card's on file in this bitch. Yall better act like you got some motherfuckin' sense!"

Four stallions strolled in, each wearing a different color coat with matching wigs. I pointed out my brother to the one who seemed to be the leader, and she nodded.

I found my bag in the corner and pulled out several thick stacks of ones. I made my way over to him and handed them over. "Go stupid, bruh. Within reason."

I realized just then that I wasn't sure if Taurus had ever even been to a strip club.

He always felt like he had to be an example for me and Isaac. After my father died, it's like a switch flipped in him. He got stern and regimented, and less of a big brother.

But as the man of the hour, he was about to let loose, and I truly hoped he had fun.

I found Isaac as the music changed to Juicy J and colorful coats went flying.

"You good?" I asked him.

"Chillin'. Ready to see some asses shaking. How bout you?"

"Tired, honestly."

The girl in the pink wig walked right up to me with that stripper smile. I was too experienced to fall for that shit, but I smiled back, my eyes falling to her legs.

Black stockings, but they only went up to the middle of her thigh. Garters hung down, catching them right in the middle. It came to me immediately that of all the variations there could ever be, those were my absolute favorites. Hands down. Shit was so sexy.

But it also came to me that what I really wanted was to see them on Electra.

"What's your name?" she asked me.

"Victor."

"You're cute, Victor. You don't look like you're having fun, though."

"You know what? This is my brother, Isaac. He's way more fun than I am."

Her attention instantly went to him. She sat him down and began her dance. On the other side of the room, Taurus was flanked by a girl in yellow and a girl in purple.

The girl in green was entertaining the rest of the guys, and I stood and watched for about two minutes before I realized I was too old for this shit.

I would have my own bachelor party one day, and I'd have fun at that one, but this shit here wasn't doing anything for me. The girls were sexy, but I wasn't moved.

I took one more look at the girl in pink, and at her lingerie, before retreating to the couch.

For the first time in my life, I experienced feeling lonely in a room full of people.

15

ELECTRA

CIARA'S FACE BORE SIGNS of distress.

"Again?" she asked.

"Again."

Her fork met her plate, then she straightened her back and squared her shoulders. "This is serious."

"I know."

"As far as I'm concerned, there's only one thing left to do."

"What?"

"Kill him."

I rolled my eyes. "Please be serious."

I'd just told her about my second attempt with Lance the other night in hopes that she'd actually pose some real solutions. I'd even brought her to her favorite lunch spot to treat her to her favorite Cobb salad and lobster roll.

"I *am* serious," she insisted.

I laughed. "Will you stop?"

"Okay," she laughed with me. "But you're not gonna like what I have to say next."

"I didn't like what you said the first time, so how much worse could it get?"

Her brow furrowed. "I have an actual solution, but I know you. You're gonna shoot it down."

"Just tell me."

"What's his name, again? Your coworker?"

"Victor."

She picked up her phone. "Last name?"

"Jackson. What are you doing?"

She shrugged as her fingers typed furiously, her devilish smile growing into Grinch territory.

"Oh. Oh. Yeah." She nodded at her phone screen. "My instincts were correct."

"Meaning...?"

She looked up at me. "Girl, you need to fuck that man. Post haste."

"I cannot *stand* him. And I'm not being dramatic, here. I don't like that negro."

"Okay, but look at him." She shoved her phone in my face. "Look at that face!"

I reared back, shaking my head, refusing to look at it. "I know what he looks like. I have to see it every day."

"And you *still* hate him? You're a better woman than me, girl."

"Okay. Let's focus. I need a solution to my problem."

"That *is* the solution. He stole your orgasm from you with all his bullshit, so...steal it back. This isn't rocket science."

"Whatever. Since you like him so much, I'll hook you up. How about that?"

But even as the words left my lips, I knew they were a lie. Her raised eyebrow told me she was considering it, or at the very least, picturing it, and my muscles tensed at the sight of it. Which was ridiculous, but also, educational.

I hate focus groups.

People talk over each other, jockey for position, tell you what you want to hear instead of giving you the information you need, and frankly, they're boring.

But they're a necessary evil in this business.

You can glean information from anonymous surveys, but there's something about the atmosphere of the group that elicits more candid information.

Today, the Candyman and I were working side-by-side to get this done. We had several deliverables due next week, and I, for one, couldn't have been happier. It meant less talking and more typing. Alone. Without having to smell his cologne or be assaulted by flashbacks of his lustful stare every time I looked at his face.

"Felicity, it seems like you had something you wanted to say."

Today's topic was work environment, and the behavior of our ten attendees was pretty indicative of typical workplace dynamics. I took copious notes on that, while Victor was in charge of the recording.

"Oh, my bad," Jason said. "Didn't mean to talk over you."

He had, though, and everyone knew it. Jason was a best-in-class mansplainer.

Felicity cleared her throat. "Yes, I was just saying that I do think the climate can sometimes be rough for people like me."

Matt snickered.

"Matt, did you have a response to that?" I said, ignoring the response he'd just given.

He shrugged. "I don't know. It's like, is this about to devolve into some DEI nonsense? If so, I have more important work I could be doing."

"Well—"

"You don't think listening to your coworker's experience is important?" Victor said. "Why might that be, Matt?"

I was probably the only person in the room who caught the carefully controlled command in that question. After having been around him, I was learning him a little.

Matt's body stiffened at the challenge. "It's just...annoying. It's like 'wah, wah, somebody was mean to me.' Okay, we get it. Jesus."

Felicity's face flushed red.

"To be clear," I began, "you're complaining that your coworker is complaining? In what way is your complaint different from hers?"

His eyes narrowed. "Don't put words in my mouth."

"You might wanna watch your tone," Victor said. "Let's keep this professional. And respectful."

"How was what I said disrespectful?"

This time, *my* body tensed. Victor was a reasonable man, but from what I'd seen, he didn't suffer fools, which Matt appeared to be.

I kept my eyes straight ahead, watching Matt. Victor's voice, deep and even, sounded out next to me.

"Ms. Montrose asked you a question and you responded with an unnecessary order. And I didn't care for your tone."

Matt snickered. "See, this is what I mean. Everybody's so sensitive."

It seemed like we all fidgeted at the same time while we waited for Victor to respond. He wouldn't do or say anything unprofessional…at least, I hoped he wouldn't.

My heart pounded.

I wondered if I should step in.

"I want to apologize to the rest of you," Victor said. I whipped my head to my right. He had my full attention now.

"I'm truly sorry for the interruption," he continued. "Matt needed attention, and he decided to troll this discussion to get it. I asked him a question expecting a reasonable answer, but as we saw, he's incapable. I think he's done, though, so we'll go ahead and finish up. Unless…" he looked at Matt. "Anything else?"

Matt's shoulders slumped, and a weak shake of his head followed.

Victor looked over at me. "Floor is yours."

The rest of the focus group went on without incident. Matt's angry stares and tense body language notwithstanding, I was satisfied with what we got. After I ushered the group out of the door, I turned to Victor.

"What was that?"

"What?" His genuine confusion would have been funny if this wasn't such a dire situation.

"I appreciate you looking out, but please try not to lose sight of the fact that the check hasn't cleared yet."

He shrugged. "He wasn't gon' do shit."

"That's not the point."

"So I was supposed to let him disrespect you?"

"I guess I don't see why you care."

"I don't," he snapped. "You're on my team, so…" he trailed off.

"So, what?"

His dark eyes held mine as he drew in a deep breath. "A long time ago, way back in undergrad, we read this article in one of my classes. It was about black women in tech. Something about it stuck with me."

I seated myself in my chair and crossed my legs. I didn't miss the way his eyes dropped to follow the movement before coming back to rest on my face.

"What did it say?"

"The gist of it was something about the burden of being a double minority in a space that's unfriendly to black folks and to women. Yall are both, so you get hit twice."

The language he used was too specific to match his performative nonchalance.

"That's true," I said.

"I know. And when we got forced onto this project together, I looked up some more articles. Just to see if anything's changed, I guess. And it hasn't. So I figured the least I could do was look out and help protect you. Since, you know, you're on my team."

"Wow. I—"

"And don't take that to mean I don't think you can handle yourself," he rushed out. "I know you can. Look how you treat me."

I chuckled at that.

"But I know it can be different when you're face-to-face with the problem, so...anyway, just know no matter how I feel about you personally, I'm not gon' let nobody up in here treat you any kind of way. Only *I* can treat you any kind of way."

I burst out laughing. I was mad about it, too, because it felt like ceding territory. And he had the nerve to smile about it, like he was enjoying it.

Can't have that.

I cleared my throat and straightened up. "I guess it doesn't hurt to have you looking out around here."

"Exactly." He was quiet for a moment. "But for the record, not everything that hurts is bad."

"Excuse me?"

"You didn't hear me?"

"I did. I'm not sure I understood, though."

"Seems pretty straightforward to me."

The ambiguity was too calculated to be a mistake, but that's exactly what made it impossible to address.

I turned my chair to face my desk, swallowing hard as I willed myself to ignore it.

And my body's response to it.

16

Vic

Steam rose around me as hot water ran down my back and lapped at my feet before circling the drain. With it, it carried the evidence of my growing state of discontent.

I dreamed of her last night.

The velvety soft skin. The faint, sweet smell of honey. Her hair brushing the side of my face. The taste of her lips. Handfuls of succulent flesh. She was on top of me. I remembered that clearly. Where we were and how we got there still remained a mystery.

Her moans were so loud and visceral, I would have sworn on the good book that she was really here. That she was actually riding me. Pleasing me. Pleasing herself.

But it was a dream.

The arousal was real, though. So was the orgasm.

It was so intense, my dick was still throbbing when I woke up. I lay there for a while before I finally opened my eyes. I stared around my empty room as the first rays of sun beamed through the crevices between my blinds like beacons of reality. Disappointment dropped on me like a thousand-pound boulder, but as I lay there, the lust didn't subside. If anything, it escalated.

Now came the cleanup.

I washed quickly, hoping to avoid shower thoughts of her. I threw on a t-shirt and sweatpants, gathered up my sheets, and put them in the laundry. After I made the bed with fresh linens, I checked the time. I had about an hour to eat and meditate before I got to work.

Fuck.

She would be there.

Just when I had put that dream out of my mind.

Of all the women in all the world...I had to dream about *her*. The countdown was still on, but mentally, I was already bursting out of the starting block. That nut was like the pop of the starter pistol. A nigga was off to the races now. And she was my prize.

My phone rang.

"What's up, T?"

"Savannah's water broke," he said breathlessly.

"Oh, shit. It's happening?"

"Yeah. Listen, I need you to go grab Naya for me."

"I got work."

"Can you call out? You're the only one I got."

It was true. My mama didn't drive, and Isaac...that nigga's license was always either suspended or lost.

"Alright, man. I got you. Text me the address of the school and the hospital."

"'Preciate you."

"Aye, how's Savannah holding up?"

"So far, so good, man. She's a trooper."

"Alright, I'll see y'all soon."

It wasn't like me to miss work. With no family, I've always been the one who comes in early, stays late, works holidays if I need to. This right here was unprecedented.

But I didn't mind if it meant avoiding *her*.

Because the only thing worse than wanting a woman is knowing you can't have her.

17

Electra

Victor wasn't here when I got here.

Strange.

He always beat me in.

I looked at his empty chair and smiled. To be quite honest, I'd been annoyed that he had that to hold over my head if he wanted to.

It wasn't exactly a fair fight, in my view. Women have to work a lot harder to look professional, at least in my industry. I've read the statistics. I know my shit. Professionalism, for women, is based in part on makeup, the right clothes, the right shoes, the right handbag, and I could go on an entire tangent about hair. So the fact that Victor, a man, can roll out of bed and throw on a suit says less about me and my work ethic and more about gender in the workplace.

So yes, I was happy I beat him today.

I take my little wins where I can get them.

But by the time I got to the bottom of my Starbucks, I was feeling a little less victorious and a lot less smug.

He was thirty minutes late at this point, which was cause for alarm. Or, it *would* have been if I cared about his wellbeing. Which I didn't. We had work to do, and he was absent. And he hadn't called.

I spun around. "Hey, Nora."

"Yes, love?"

"Have you heard from Victor? It's not like him to be late."

Nora removed her glasses and nodded. "He called me a little while ago. His sister-in-law went into labor."

"And he called *you*?"

"Yes..."

"And you didn't say anything to me?"

Her eyebrows rose slowly.

"I mean...I didn't mean...I don't know. Never mind."

I sat and mulled that over, wishing I could rewind and scrap the last few moments of our conversation. Because if *I* heard the desperation in my voice, she must have heard it, too. I hadn't known the woman long, but in my mind, she already occupied the same spaces aunties do, in that she didn't have to verbally express the fact that she was looking out for me from a comfortable distance for me to feel it. But that also meant she would drag me if the need arose.

And I was looking kinda needy right now.

"I should send something!" I said a little too loudly. "Right?"

Nora shrugged.

"Just...you know. As a polite gesture. It's what my mother would do. She's a stickler for that kind of stuff. Etiquette, I mean." I chuckled nervously. "Like thank you notes. Oh God, I can't even begin to tell you how many times she—"

"How long has this been going on?" Nora interrupted.

"What? Thank you notes?"

Her arms crossed. Her chin dipped. That was it. That was the pose. I'd activated her.

"What, Nora? How long has *what* been going on?"

"This little love affair."

"Excuse me?"

Her lips pursed. "Girl, please. You think I'm stupid?"

"Of course not. I'm just confused."

"Confused?" She laughed. "Chile...do you think I think *you're* stupid?"

My shoulders slumped in defeat. "No."

"Mm hm. Yall sit up in here all day every day acting like kindergarten kids on the playground. I'm surprised he ain't pulled your hair and pushed you down yet."

"That's not what's going on here, trust me. We have history. Unpleasant history."

"Well, I'm sure all the denial ain't helpin' matters. I've been waiting for one of y'all to just come out and admit it already."

"Nothing to admit."

She shot me a look.

"I'm serious, Nora. And listen, I apologize if the tension has made you uncomfortable, or in any way contributed to a hostile work environment for you."

She sucked her teeth. "Can you turn that robot off? I wanna talk to Electra."

I burst out laughing. "Would you please stop dragging me? Just for a minute?"

"I will not. I'm sick of y'all."

"Have you given *him* this speech?"

"This ain't a speech. It's a cry for help. I'm tired!"

I laughed again. "I'm sorry."

She shook her head. "Don't apologize to me. Apologize to yourself for the deprivation. Shoot, if I was fifteen years younger—"

"Oh, we know," I said. "It's very obvious."

"And I'm not ashamed. Not like you seem to be."

"I told you…it's complicated."

Her face softened mercifully, letting me know the dragging was over. For now. "You wanna talk about it?"

I didn't. Not with her. Not with anybody.

"I'm gonna send some flowers to the hospital," I said instead. "Should I put your name on them?"

"Nope," she answered quickly. "That's all you, sweetheart."

I shrugged a shoulder as I swiveled in my seat, turning back to my laptop to make the purchase.

It was the polite thing to do. Endra Montrose really was a stickler about these things, and she'd passed that on to me. He was a coworker, and a teammate, and his family was experiencing something important and celebratory. Of *course* I should send something.

And it had nothing to do with my conversation with Ci, which had been on loop inside my head ever since.

You need to fuck that man.

I shook my head as I pulled out my debit card.

Because how would that even work? As marginally tolerable as he'd been of late, I still hated him. H-Town and Martin taught me there's a thin line between love and hate, but are there points on that line where sex exists?

I couldn't see it.

I pressed purchase and closed out, eager to get back to my work.

18

Vic

I walked up in Baker Academy on a mission.

The lady in the front office didn't give a fuck, though. Old girl gave me the business. I was on the list of approved contacts to pick up Naya, but she still insisted on making two copies of my driver's license and getting verbal confirmation from her mother, Amber.

I guess that's how they do it at these bougie ass private schools.

Matter of fact…this seemed like exactly the kind of school Electra Fucking Montrose would have attended.

Once we got on the road, my niece talked my ear off. She was a chatterbox, that one, but I did what any good uncle would do, and that's listen.

"And then Jayden pushed me off the swing right when I was getting off, and I fell on my knees. My mommy was mad when I came home with dirt on my tights, but it wasn't my fault, Uncle V. So we had to go buy new tights, and then she said she was gonna talk to Jayden's mom, but I don't know if she did."

"How old is this boy?" I said, my blood boiling.

"He's eight like me."

"Well, here's the thing, Ny. Unlike your mom, Uncle V don't do no talking. What's the boy's last name?"

Her eyes got big. "Are you gonna call him?"

"I might."

"I don't want you to call him."

"He pushed you off the swing, baby girl."

"He was just playing around. And Aria, that's my best friend, Aria said he did that because he likes me. But I don't like him, because he smells like bologna."

I glanced at her little face in the rearview mirror and found a copy paste of my brother's, only adorable and innocent. My protective instinct was on overdrive, but I kept my voice even.

"Don't listen to Aria. Boys aren't supposed to be mean when they like you. They're supposed to be nice to you. They should be nice anyway, but *especially* if they like you."

I'd pulled my share of beaded braids on playgrounds back in my day, so I knew what I was talking about. But I knew better now.

Or did I?

Before I let my mind wander to *her* again, I briefly wondered what that little motherfucker could possibly be doing to come to school smelling like bologna.

Before I could ask, Ny said, "He's my friend, Uncle V."

Her little voice pricked me, and so did her defense of Oscar Meyer.

"Alright, Ny. If you don't want me to call him, I respect that. Does your dad know?"

"I don't know. I didn't tell him."

That was probably for the best. Taurus would pull up, for sure. And Isaac? Isaac's been to jail. He would go back for his niece.

But the boy was eight. And we were hypocrites. I wondered how many uncles wanted to pull up on me back in the day.

That was an uncomfortable thought.

"You excited to meet your baby brother?"

A shrill, "Yes!" pierced my eardrum. "I helped them paint his room. We painted his name on the wall yesterday."

"For real? What's his name?"

"I can't tell you."

She said it immediately and with so much conviction, it felt like she'd been briefed.

"Really, Ny? Not even your favorite uncle?"

She scrunched up her nose. "I have two favorite uncles."

"Yeah, yeah." I pulled into the parking garage, grabbing a ticket from the mouth of the machine. "Go ahead and get your stuff together."

After I parked, me and Naya walked hand-in-hand to the elevator. The nurse at the desk pointed us to the waiting area closest to room four-thirty-eight. We set off down the long hallway, and the further we walked, the tighter her little grip got on my hand.

Just before we reached the waiting area, I stopped and got down to eye-level with her.

"Are you nervous?" I asked her.

She shook her head.

"Because it's okay to be nervous. This is a big change for you. But you should know that your dad, and Savannah, and the whole family, we love you and we'll always love you. That won't ever change."

"I know," she said, and I was relieved that she'd been briefed on that, too.

"It's just..." she trailed off. "I don't get to live with my brother."

Her eyes welled up with tears. "My mommy said I'll still live at her house. When I go to see my daddy, and then I leave, I have to leave him, too."

I grabbed her in my arms and held her as her little body shook with sobs.

"It's okay, Ny." I gently rubbed her back. "It's gonna be okay."

But, would it? This was a situation that couldn't be helped, it seemed to me.

I held her until she pulled away, then wiped her little nose with my finger and walked her over to the waiting area where my mother, Isaac, and Savannah's mother sat waiting.

We all exchanged hugs, then sat down to wait. I wondered how things were going at work. Part of me wanted to call, but I decided it was best to stay distracted.

Taurus poked his head out and looked around until he spotted us.

"Ms. Johnson, you wanna go see her?"

Savannah's mother jumped up. "Of course."

He hugged her as she passed, then walked over to me.

"Hey, Papa. How's it going?"

Taurus wiped his forehead. "Slow, man. It's her first baby. She's a trooper, but I'm kinda worried."

"About what?"

"The nurse said she's progressing slow. She's in a lot of pain, too. Shit got me on edge."

"It's *supposed* to hurt, though, right? I mean, damn, that shit sounds insensitive, but you know what I mean."

But he hadn't heard me, it seemed. "She said she didn't want an epidural. She wants to do it naturally."

"And epidural is...what exactly?"

"The pain paralysis drug they put in your back so you don't feel shit."

"Oh. Shit. Sign me up. Who would wanna—"

"That's what she wants, man. I don't know. The punk ass doctor be poppin' in and out when he feels like it."

I took in the expression on his face, and the way his body was coiled up tight. "It's okay, man. Relax. I'm sure she's okay. It took a minute for Ny to get here, from what I remember. Right?"

He nodded. "I'm trippin', huh?"

"A little."

"I'm..." he trailed off, shaking his head. "I don't know why, but I'm worried."

"About what?"

"That woman is my whole world, man. I can't lose her."

"Where is this coming from?"

He went to answer when Savannah's mother popped her head out. "Taurus? She's asking for you. Bring Naya in, too."

He nodded. "Aye, I gotta—"

"Go," I told him. "We'll be here, man. Tell Savannah we're out here."

As he walked away, I quickly decided that today wasn't the day to bring up anything me and Naya had talked about. He had too much on his mind as it was.

Little Christopher Taurus Jackson only made us wait another four hours before he dove into the world headfirst and made us all fall in love.

Savannah was fine, so my brother was fine, which put the rest of us at ease. He'd always set the tempo in the family. When I left, all was well, but not with me.

It was the end of the day. *She* might not even be there, was my thinking. There was a good chance I'd have the office to myself, in fact, so I made a last minute U-turn and headed in the direction of StarTech.

As soon as I rounded the corner to walk in the door of our office, I smelled her scent.

Honey.

I heard music, too. A man crooning.

She looked up at the sound of my footsteps. "What are you doing here?"

She quickly cut off the music, which had been coming from her laptop.

I looked around. "Uh, I work here."

She rolled her eyes. "I meant, this late."

"I don't like missing work, so I came to work. Is that alright with you?"

"How did it go?"

I sighed. "It went fine. Baby's healthy."

"Boy or girl?"

"Boy." I flopped down onto my chair. "I'm tired as hell. That shit takes a lot outta you."

"What does?"

"Childbirth."

"Oh, right. Did you have a c-section, or did you do it natural?"

She followed that up with a laugh at her own corny ass joke.

"Obviously, my sister-in-law gave birth, but I'm talking about the emotion of it. Seeing my brother like that."

"Like what?"

"He was worried. I'm pretty sure she was okay the whole time, but he was on edge."

"Yeah. I get that. Childbirth and black women…" she trailed off.

"You gonna finish that?"

"You don't know?"

I shrugged.

"Black women are more likely to die in childbirth. Like, way more."

"That's fucked up."

"That's an understatement."

"Right. Why, though?"

She let out a sigh that was tinged with exhaustion. "Racism in healthcare."

"Oh. Well, now it all makes sense. How he was acting, I mean. He was on one."

"Well, good. Black women need protectors." She peered at me. "You alright?"

"Yeah. Told you I'm tired. What'd I miss?"

She shut down her computer, slamming her laptop shut with a flourish. "Unfortunately for you, I'm headed out. You'll have to get the notes from a classmate."

I chuckled. "Got another date?"

Her head swiveled. "Why do you care?"

"How many times I gotta tell you, I don't? Either I'm making small talk, or I'm entertaining myself."

She stood to load up her things in her bag, giving me a full presentation. Fitted black dress, plain black stockings, black patent leather heels. Pearls in her ears and at her neck. Not a single hair out of place. The woman was effortlessly impeccable. I wondered if she knew how fucking enticing she was, or that erecting a wall of perfection only made a man like me wanna tear it down.

"If you *must* know," she said, "I'm going to happy hour."

"Where at?"

She sighed. "Five o'clock."

"Over at BillCo?"

"*Yes.*"

"I'ma tag along."

Her top lip curled as she said, "I don't remember inviting you."

"You didn't. I'm still coming."

She shrugged, but it was a pretense. "It's a big place. We don't have to sit together."

That was true, but it didn't matter. I wasn't going for social reasons. She was gonna catch me up whether she wanted to or not.

And after that...maybe I could make something shake.

I beat her to the bar, taking my seat and bobbing my head to the music while the bartender approached me. Five o'clock was always a vibe.

I gave him a nod. "What's up, bruh? Yall got Laphroaig?"

"Yep."

"Rocks. And lemme get the driest white you got."

"You got it, boss."

I sat back on my stool and looked around me, surprised by how packed the place was. But that was cool. No open tables would mean she had to sit with me.

When she walked in a few minutes later, I stared at her legs, and those stockings, and had a change of heart.

Work could wait.

19

Electra

Victor was quieter than usual.

"You sure you're alright?" I asked him. "I mean, I don't care, but you seem like you have a lot on your mind."

He turned his glass up. I watched his Adam's apple as he swallowed, unnerved by its prominence and my interest in it.

"My niece," he said once he finished. "She's only eight. She was upset because she won't get to live with her brother. My brother had her from his first marriage," he added.

"Poor baby."

"Yeah. It'll work itself out, I guess. I just hated seeing her all upset like that. She's a baby herself."

"You sound like a good uncle."

He shrugged.

"I'm impressed by your empathy. Well, not impressed. Surprised, maybe."

He frowned at me. "Is that your way of comforting me? Cuz you suck at that shit."

I laughed. "Why would I comfort you?"

"Right. You wouldn't. Back to business." His eyes dropped to my legs. "What did I miss?"

I waited until his attention returned to my face to answer, "You couldn't just find out tomorrow?"

"I don't like being behind." He chuckled. "At least not at work."

I nearly choked on the wine I'd just sipped, but I recovered quickly, then took a moment to fill him on the day's events.

When I finished, he signaled the bartender. "Any problems with ol' boy?"

"Who?"

"That punk ass motherfucker from the other day. Alex?"

"Oh, Ellis?"

"Yeah."

"Nope. On his best behavior. I guess I owe that to you."

He shrank back a little and shook his head. "Nah, you don't owe me anything. Like I told you before, just making sure everybody on my team gets the proper respect."

I nodded. "Thanks. But also? I'm not on your team. You're on *my* team."

A devilish smile crossed his lips just then, and I turned away quickly.

"Drunk In Love" came on over the speaker system. I was already relaxed, but between the alcohol and the music, and, honestly, the *company*, I was also feeling ever so slightly turned on. And cautious, because when I drink too much, I end up with loose lips. The last thing I wanted was to talk too much in front of Victor, of all people. To slip up and say something that might expose my state of mind.

I promised myself I'd stop at two.

I let my eyes wander around the crowded restaurant and came to a disturbing revelation.

Victor was the best looking man in the room. In fact, he was probably the best looking man within a fifty-mile radius. And that fact was evidenced by the stares he was getting from damn near every woman in the room. It was...irritating.

You need to fuck that man.

I mean...because if I didn't, somebody up in here would.

The bartender returned just then.

"Lemme get another one," Victor said, turning to me. "You want another?"

"Yes, please."

He smiled. "So tell me something."

I raised my eyebrows.

"Did your date not go well?"

"Why are you so interested in my date?"

He chuckled. "How many times do I have to answer that question?"

"I'm not interested in being your entertainment."

The smile died on his lips as his face went serious. "Then satisfy my curiosity."

Something about the way he said that made my skin prickle. And *satisfy* was ironic given my current state of frustration.

"Why would I do that?"

He swiveled on his stool to face me directly. It was like being hit in the face with a high beam light. My cheeks heated.

I cleared my throat. "What makes you think it didn't go well?"

"You came in that next day all agitated," he said. "I'm just sayin'. Usually when I go on a date, I'm chill afterwards."

"Did it ever occur to you that my feelings were completely unrelated to my date?"

"That's why I'm asking. When you bring your bad date energy to the office, it affects me."

"Wow." I chuckled, in spite of myself. "If anything, my bad energy is *because* of you."

His dark eyes narrowed as they bore into mine, and I begged myself not to let the words come pouring out of my mouth.

Don't say it.

Do not *say it.*

"I think the stress of...all of this—"

He leaned in. "What's all of this?"

"The tension and hostility. I feel like it's taking a toll on me."

I shouldn't have, but I drank half of that second glass. With the last swallow, my shoulders dropped, and my thoughts became fuzzy around the edges. But I still had the presence of mind to remind myself.

Stop talking.

"My date was fine," I said, against the better judgment of the last remnants of my sobriety. "I've been seeing him off and on for a while."

"What's his name?"

Stop talking...

"Lance."

"Lance," he repeated. "Corny ass name."

"Whatever."

"So what's the problem with Lance?" His eyes flickered over me. "He ain't hit it right?"

A laugh burst out of me before I could stop it. "That's so inappropriate."

"But you laughed."

"Because. You're..."

"Too charming to resist?"

I brought my eyes back to his face, which was fixed in an expression of jubilant curiosity. "I was gonna say obnoxious in an amusing way, but okay. Sure."

"Answer the question."

"Are you always this pushy?"

"I prefer to think of it as aggressive."

"That's better?"

He smiled slyly. "You don't like aggressive men?"

I blinked several times as my brain tried to catch up. I wasn't sure if it was the alcohol or my attraction to him, or maybe both, but I was flustered.

"Don't you have your own dates to worry about?" was all I could manage to say.

"Since you asked, yeah. I had one last week."

My brown eyes flashed bright green upon hearing that, but I quickly recovered with, "What happened, she didn't hit that right?"

He burst out laughing. "That was so corny."

"But you laughed."

He nodded. "Touché. Now, back to Lance. What he do wrong?"

Stop talking.

"Nothing. That's the thing. He did the same things he's always done, but it just didn't..."

He frowned, then his chiseled face relaxed in recognition. I knew immediately that I'd said too much, cursing that second glass of wine, which...when the hell had I finished it?

"Damn," he said. "You really..." he trailed off, shaking his head.

"What?"

"You're really tellin' me your business right now."

I shrugged a shoulder. "I talk too much when I drink. Don't feel special."

"I *am* special."

I rolled my eyes at that. "All narcissists say that."

"Oh, now I'm a narcissist? You learn that on TikTok?"

"Whatever, Victor."

His eyes grazed me in a way that made my body tingle. "So he couldn't get you there, huh?"

"Doesn't matter."

"I disagree."

"Well, it matters, but not to *you*."

His tongue appeared and ran slowly between his lips. "I still disagree."

Stop. Talking.

"You know what?" I sighed. "You're actually right."

"I know."

"But not for the reason you think."

"Then why am I right?"

I picked up a napkin and fidgeted with it, tearing little lines in the edges. "I think…I think it's because I'm so stressed out…from working with you." I stared down at my fingers. "You…you stole it."

"I *stole* it?" He slowly dissolved into quiet laughter, his eyes locked on mine. "Wait, so it's my fault you can't bust a n—"

"Ugh! You're so vulgar."

He put his hands up. "My bad, Miss Priss. It's my fault you…" his voice lowered. "Can't have an orgasm?"

"Yeah. Basically. I never had this problem before I started working with you."

"Damn. I'm sorry to hear that."

"No you're not."

"I am," he insisted. "I mean, aside from the ridiculous fact that you're blaming me for it, I wouldn't wish that on my worst enemy. Which is you, I guess."

I shrugged and set my ribboned napkin back in its place.

He put a hand on the back of my stool, leaning in a little closer and lowering his voice to say, "You should probably get that treated."

I rolled my eyes. "Yeah, I'll make an appointment right away."

His eyes fell to my legs again. I shivered, hoping he didn't notice.

"No appointments necessary. I take walk-ins."

Slow on the uptake again, it took me a few seconds to say, "Are you insane?"

He brought his eyes back to mine. "Who better to give it to you than the one who stole it in the first place?"

"That was a joke, Victor." I looked away, mumbling, "For the most part."

"Am I laughing?"

I stared at the oak bar and felt myself weakening.

I hated this man. So very much. But at this moment, parts of me liked him. A lot. I'd tried my best to ignore it, but I felt swollen between my thighs. Full and hard and hot. I knew if I didn't put a stop to this, the flood wasn't far behind.

"Listen," he said. "We're consultants, right? We solve problems. It sounds to me like you have a serious problem on your hands, Electra."

I brought my eyes to his, not at all surprised to see that same face I saw in the conference room a few weeks ago. Beast mode. Was I really going to let this man shark me out of my panties?

"Strictly business," he continued. "I just did a needs assessment, and I have a recommendation just for you."

God help me. All I had to do was get up and leave. Or change the subject. Better yet, I could just say no and leave it at that.

"What do you recommend?" was what I chose instead.

His perfect lips parted. He leaned closer. "One night with me."

I took in a deep, shaky breath. We'd never been this close before. Close enough to kiss.

"But I don't like you."

He chuckled. "Do you honestly think that'll matter to you when I have your eyes rolling back?"

Good lord.

"If it makes you feel any better," he continued, as if he hadn't said enough, "we don't have to like each other after, either."

"How does *that* work?"

He leaned in even closer, lowering his voice, his full lips brushing my ear. "You've never fucked somebody you can't stand?"

I swallowed hard as the flood began in earnest, pushing past my emotional levees and sweeping away my objections as it settled between my legs, leaving me wet with desire.

"Can't say that I have."

He nodded as his eyes caressed my face. "I have. No feelings. No love. No affection. Just you getting yours."

It didn't surprise me that a man like him had experience with this given how easy he was to hate.

"Am I supposed to believe there's nothing in this for you?"

To my relief, he leaned back, giving me space to breathe air that wasn't tinged with his cologne. My head began to clear again, until he spoke.

"I'm not gonna pretend like I won't enjoy it," he admitted, then teasingly added, "Is it alright with you if I enjoy it?"

"None of this is alright with me. What if—"

"How many do you want?"

"What? What do you mean?"

His nostrils flared. "You know exactly what I mean. How many?"

"I guess...however many...um..."

"I'll go until you tell me to stop." His eyes fell to my lips. "Or beg me. I don't have a preference."

His voice was huskier. Deeper. My nipples hardened.

"I...I can't believe we're talking about this," I said quietly.

"It's more of a negotiation. No feelings, remember?"

I nodded. It was all I could do.

He sat up straight and cleared his throat. "So that's the offer, Electra. Think it over and let me know what you decide. There's no clock."

"Oh. I thought you meant tonight."

His lips curved into a sly smile. "I meant whenever. But since you're clearly very thirsty, we can put a rush on it."

"You're real close to talking yourself out of this, Victor. Tread lightly."

"That's what your mouth says. Your body's saying different. *Again.*"

As I watched him finish his drink, I cursed my thin white silk blouse. Caught slipping again. No wonder he was acting so smug.

"That's just biology," I defended. "My mind is stronger. Don't ever forget that."

"Yes, ma'am." He grinned. "Should I get the check, or do you wanna keep arguing? I know how important foreplay is."

I shook my head. "You're the worst. Your place or mine?"

He pulled out a stunning brown leather wallet, pulling out a fifty and tossing it on the bar.

"I'm fifteen minutes away. Where are you?"

"Five."

He stood. "I'm following you."

20

ELECTRA

"Nice place."

I tossed my keys into the gold leaf bowl on my hall table. "Thanks."

"Not as nice as mine, though."

I ignored his teasing grin as I turned behind me to lock the front door. "Where's your bathroom? I wanna wash my hands."

"Follow me. You can use the master."

I led him down the short hallway, keeping my walk slow and measured. My buzz was wearing off, and in hindsight, I realized he'd controlled the conversation at the bar. It was time to flip that dynamic back to the baseline. *I* was in control, not him.

We entered the master bedroom. "Right there," I said, pointing to the door on the right. Without a word, he retreated to my bathroom while I sat on the edge of my bed, desperate to catch my breath.

I wasn't under duress when I agreed to this. I knew with a clear head that I wanted this. *Bad*. But I wasn't convinced I'd come out of this unscathed. Sex had always held meaning for me, even when I wished it hadn't. Could I really stay detached after this? I wasn't confident. The last thing I needed was to fall for a man I didn't like or trust.

He walked out of my bathroom with his tie loosened, looking like pure, unadulterated sex.

Yeah.

This was the right decision.

I squeezed my thighs together to quell the needy ache between them.

He stopped in front of me and stared down. "You ready?"

"Just like that?"

"Ain't no romance here, Electra. You need to decide if you're cool with that, cuz if not..."

"I am. Um, is there anything else I need to know about this whole situation?"

His hand went to his tie. I watched him slowly loosen it the rest of the way, and I got the distinct feeling he knew I liked that.

"In my experience, it can get real intense. And I might get aggressive."

My mouth filled with saliva. "Do I need a safe word?"

He chuckled as he pulled his tie from around his neck. "What you know about that?"

"I know enough to ask if I need one."

"You don't. I won't hurt you unless you want me to." He shrugged himself out of his suit jacket. "We done talking?"

My mind was racing. "And after, we pretend like it never happened, right?"

"Absolutely."

"And you're clear on the fact that this is just...it's just sex. In fact, we're doing this for science."

His features formed into a frown, which, oddly enough, only made him more handsome. "What are you talking about right now?"

"Never mind." I took a deep breath. "I'm ready."

He held out his jacket, and I stared at it like it might come alive and strangle me, my eyes shifting between it and its owner. It was certainly very nice, but I couldn't figure out what he wanted.

"Hang this up for me," he said. "Please."

"Hang it on the door," I snapped. "This isn't romantic, remember? You don't get all that."

He nodded. "Fair enough."

Okay, but then this man walked into my damn closet and took a hanger, hanging up his jacket among my dresses. At that moment, I realized I'd have no problem detaching afterward. He was annoying as hell.

He waltzed back in and went right to his knees in front of me. Goose bumps prickled on my skin as he slid my heels off my feet and placed them neatly next to the bed. My heart raced. My mouth went dry.

It was happening.

He rubbed his hands up and down my calves, staring at the stockings that covered them. He did that a lot.

His hands moved up until they were gripping my hips.

"Lift up for me."

His voice was gruff and hard, and I liked that. I lifted myself, waiting while he hooked his fingers in the waistband of my tights and pulled them down.

His fingers grazed my skin on the way to my ankles, where he relieved me of both my stockings and my panties. I shivered in anticipation.

His fingers circled my ankles just before he pulled me forward a few inches, which served the dual purpose of pushing my skirt up and putting my bare pussy in his face.

When he spread my thighs, I watched his eyes as they zeroed in on what was in front of him. His jaw clenched. His pupils dilated. His chest rose and fell faster than it did a minute before. His nostrils flared as his eyes raised to meet mine.

"Does your pussy always get this wet for men you hate?"

"I wouldn't know. You're the first."

With his eyes back on my center, he grinned. I put my palms behind me on the bed and waited, bracing myself. He leaned in, took a long, deep breath, then pressed his mouth against my lips.

I gasped quietly. Another soft kiss followed, then another. I squirmed, shifting my hips, my body hungry for more. But I had to remain in control.

"Are you always this tender with women you hate?"

In lieu of an answer, he raised his eyes again, locking them on my face. With his fingers, he parted my lower lips. His tongue snaked out, long and pink, and licked an agonizingly slow path from my taint to the top of my clit.

My fingers seized, balling into fists, making mountainous peaks on top of my comforter. He wouldn't break his stare, and I refused to let him have control, so I stared back, feeling helpless as he teased my clit with the tip of his tongue. Over and over again, he flicked it carelessly like it was a mere toy he was using to amuse himself. I thought I even saw a mischievous gleam in his eye. He was daring me to relinquish control, which made me grit my teeth as I held back the moans gathering in my throat.

I was doing well until he closed his lips around my clit and French kissed it like he'd just brought it home at the end of a date. It was *so* erotic, and I hated him for that, because I couldn't manage my response anymore. My eyes rolled back, my head dropped back between my shoulders, and my lips parted, allowing, "Oh, God," to sneak out of my mouth.

"Mm hm."

Ugh. So cocky. So smug.

But I couldn't lie to myself about the fact that he'd earned the right.

My thighs shook. My heart thundered in my chest. His tongue felt *so* good against my sensitive flesh. I was losing it, but willingly, now. Enthusiastically. Because this time, I knew I would have no problem finishing. He was giving back what he'd stolen from me, and he was good at it, and I hated him, but at least the night wouldn't end in disappointment.

"*Fuck....*" My hips began to move to his rhythm, my fingers finding a home on top of his head. A few moments later, my eyes squeezed shut as my body went rigid in preparation for the climax. It hit me hard and fast, ripping through my lower body with carnal abandon. I let out a keening cry, and my fingers gripped his head so hard I was sure he'd protest. But he didn't, and even if he had, it wouldn't have mattered. I was *gone*.

How had I been living without this? It was almost criminal. This was life. This was medicine. It was sun and water and oxygen. I was alive again.

Moments ticked by, measured by my heartbeats. Aftershocks. Moans. Trembles. Then came the quiet calm. The pleasant fatigue. The sense of satisfaction. I was done for the evening. He was still here, sitting patiently between my legs, but I didn't need him anymore. And that was a relief.

A finger slid inside me.

My head popped up just in time to see him ease a second finger in.

"What are you doing?" I moaned.

He looked up at me. "I'm giving you another one."

"I'm good, Victor."

He bit his lip, his dark eyes narrowing as he regarded me. "When I asked you how many you wanted, you gave me a vague answer. You're about to learn from that mistake."

Before I could respond, his fingers moved slowly and sensually inside me. In the face of his failure to listen to me, I went to roll my eyes, but the pleasure of his handiwork was like a sedative, making my eyelids too heavy to do anything other than flutter to a close.

"I'll stop if you want me to," I heard him say quietly. "Do you want me to stop?"

I shook my head, but he stopped anyway.

"Tell me." The gruff demand caught me off guard. More controlling behavior. He was so aggravating.

But the cum-starved girl inside me moaned, "Don't stop."

"Good girl. That wasn't so hard, was it?"

God, I hated him so much. So...so...

So...much...*ohhhhh...yessssss...*

His fingers stroked me so good, I would have crawled on my knees like a dog if he told me to.

"You hear that?"

The strain in his voice was so sexy. I heard that, and I heard what he was referring to—the sound of my wetness all over his fingers. I hadn't been finger-fucked in a while, and I can't say I'd missed it. But this? Fucking *hell*. Something about the way he touched me. The way his fingers moved. Carefully orchestrated dexterity, gently plumbing the depths of me, probing me, exploring me, searching and strumming and rotating, softly drilling to strike liquid gold once again and unleash a torrent of pleasure all over his fingers.

My body jerked as the pressure built.

So close.

"Oh God, Vic..."

Vic? Why did I call him that?

His tongue found its way back to my clit, and that question went unanswered as my mind shifted to my impending orgasm. Number two. So happy to see you. Please join us. Stay a while.

"Yes! Yes, yes, yes, fuck!" I screamed over and over as number two erupted inside me.

He let me ride the waves before removing his fingers, slowly pulling out of me while I panted my way through. I was spent, but I knew he wasn't done with me. It was time for him to get what he wanted.

And I wanted him to have it.

Not because I owed him. He'd made me feel so good, I wanted to share the wealth. We…maybe…*possibly*…had something here.

Sounds reached my ringing ears. Jangling, probably his belt buckle. Crinkling; the condom. My center throbbed with a need that surprised me given how sated I felt.

His hand wrapped around my wrist, singeing me, making me force my eyes open.

"What are you doing?"

"Come here."

He pulled me to a standing position. I balanced on shaky legs as my eyes fell to his dick, which was standing at full attention over the top of his boxers. It was impressive, size-wise. All that remained was for me to find out if he knew how to use it.

He pulled me a few feet over, then turned us around and backed me up to my desk.

"No bed," he explained.

No nudity either, I guess. I nodded and hiked up my skirt, bringing myself to rest on top of the cold wood. Without another word, he lined himself up. I wasn't sure what to do with my hands, whether to brace myself or hold onto him. As he eased himself in, I decided to hold onto him. It didn't mean anything. It was simply a matter of safety; he was sturdier than my desk.

Back and shoulder muscles bulged against my fingers as he buried himself inside me, locking into place. He stopped, sighing deeply. I stared at his face and tried to read the frown and grimace.

"I need a second," he gritted out.

"You okay?"

He shook his head. "I didn't expect you to feel this good."

I pulled my head back. "Why?"

His hooded eyes came to rest on mine. "Honestly? You don't have 'good pussy' energy."

My face twisted to register my disgust. "So you can't even be nice when your dick is in me?"

He smiled. "Say dick again."

"Shut up."

"Nah, that was sexy. Say it."

"You're an asshole. And you're real close to getting thrown out of here. See, this is why I hate you."

"Alright, okay. I apologize. What I should have said is that your pussy feels way better than I expected based on—"

"Stop talking and fuck me, Victor."

He nodded.

One deep breath later, he hooked my thigh under his arm and got a tight grip around my waist. Once he started stroking me, I forgot all about our petty argument from a moment before.

Long. Thick. Immaculate. I had to press my lips together to keep from screaming. There was no way I was gonna let on how good it was. Not after what he'd said.

Big-dicked asshole.

He wasn't as reserved, though. He'd already whispered, "*Electra...*" a couple of times. Moaned in baritone. Gritted out, "*Fuck,*" several times. It was my turn to feel smug, because maybe I was uptight sometimes. Prissy. Cold and rigid. But none of those traits have ever kept my pussy from getting wet. I was drowning him and I knew it. I did a few kegels just to hear him moan, smiling in triumph at the deep rumble of his voice in my ear.

"Don't hold back," he rasped. "I know it feels good."

"It's alright," I teased. It was only right after what he'd said.

His eyes burned into mine. "Keep playin' with me."

"I'm not. It's just okay."

His left hand went to the back of my neck. His right pushed my knee up to my shoulder as he leaned over, pushing me until I was almost lying down. With my body properly braced, he rammed into me with so much force, it knocked the wind out of me.

"Wait!" I managed to sputter, but the time allotted for waiting had apparently expired. That man commenced to longdicking me to the hilt and back, leaving me holding in my screams while I dug trenches in the skin on his back with my fingernails.

"Now what were you saying?" he demanded.

"I...I said...it's okay."

He wrapped my leg around his waist. With his right hand free now, he brought it to rest at my neck, leaning back to glare into my eyes while he stroked me.

"Quit fuckin' playin' with me, Electra." His fingers squeezed my neck. "You ain't gon' win this one."

I'd never been choked before, and I...didn't hate it. For a moment as fleeting as the wind, I was afraid, but despite not trusting this man at all in the office, I discovered I trusted him in my bedroom. With his dick inside me and his hand around my neck.

But I still wanted to win.

He hit my spot. The sensation almost sent me rocketing to another climax. A tiny whimper escaped.

But he still wasn't gonna win.

"How does it feel?"

I squeezed my eyes shut and said nothing. Number three was creeping up on me. His fingers flexed at my neck.

"Petty ass," he gritted. "I hate you too." He stroked me harder. Deeper. "I fucking hate you. Why is your pussy so good?"

His strokes grew frenzied and frantic, and I received them, holding on tight as my body grew weary from the onslaught of delicious, punishing strokes. Finally, reluctantly, then happily, I surrendered to Victor, submitting to his conquest with a strangled cry as intense contractions made me spasm uncontrollably around him.

"Yeah. There it is. Cum on my dick. Cum...on my...fuck!"

He slammed into me one last time. I screamed. He yelled. We moaned together at the peak, then gasped and panted together on the way down. I held his rigid body tightly, grateful for what he'd just given me, but as number three retreated further and further away, my hold on him loosened.

Clarity hit me like a freight train.

We'd just had *sex*.

He pulled out slowly and walked away, leaving me shivering on my desk.

I closed my eyes.

There was no coming back from this.

21

Vic

Spent, I sat on the edge of her bed and watched her fix her clothes. We hadn't spoken since we finished, and the awkward silence was killing me. I should have left right after. That was customary in these situations. But I stuck around.

"What did you mean earlier when you said we were doing this for science?"

There. The silence was broken.

She stopped moving and made a face at me. "It's kind of embarrassing."

"So?"

She tilted her head and smiled as if she'd just remembered neither one of us was invested.

"I tend to know random facts about things. I read this article recently about the orgasm gap."

"Okay, I'll bite."

She pulled the chair out and sat at her desk. Slowly, though. Carefully. That both concerned me and turned me on a little.

"Apparently, people of different races have orgasms more or less frequently," she explained. "Latinos have the most. Black folks are in the lower middle ranking."

I nodded. "Call them back and report on them three I just gave you."

She chuckled at that. "*Anyway,* they didn't give any reasons for it. I just found it interesting."

"That *is* interesting." I hung my tie around my neck. "You know something else interesting?"

"What?"

"I threw my brother a bachelor party a couple of weeks ago. There was this stripper there that kind of reminded me of you."

Her features sharpened, all traces of softness gone. "Why would you think I'd care about that?"

"My main point was gonna be about her stockings. If you hadn't noticed, I like them. On you. She had some on with these garters. That shit was so sexy. But when I was watching her, all I could think was that I wished they were on you, instead."

I shook my head. "I know that sounds crazy. I don't even know why I told you that."

"That makes two of us."

I reached into my pocket and pulled my phone out.

"Here." I walked over and offered it to her. "Put your number in there."

"Why would I give you my number?"

"Just in case Lucas takes you out again and can't get the job done. I'm available for service calls."

Laughing, she took the phone from me. "It's Lance."

"I do not give a *fuck.*"

She rolled her eyes. I watched her fingers move across the screen, then she handed it back. I texted her IT'S ME, then tucked my phone away.

I wasn't quite sure how to end the night. I'd told her we didn't have to like each other after, but goddamn. After what she'd just put on me, I didn't even know anymore. Up was down. Left was right. Shit was complicated.

Her eyes raised to meet mine. "This is the part where you get out, right?"

Okay, well, she made that pretty fucking simple.

I moved toward the door. "I'm out. Come lock up behind me."

I never looked back, and she never said a word.

My little brother opened the door to Taurus' house looking like a fucking librarian.

"I know that ain't who I think it is," I said in Big Boi's voice. "When the fuck did you get glasses?"

Isaac laughed as he dapped me up. "My eyes are fucked up, apparently."

"Nah, nigga, you just gettin' old."

"Whatever, man." He stepped aside to let me pass. "I'm younger than you."

I stared at his face and shook my head in awe. He looked so much like my father with those glasses on.

"There his ass go," Taurus called out as we walked into the living room. "Mama's in the kitchen."

"Lemme go speak."

Savannah and Taurus invited all of us over for dinner. I didn't see her, but my mama was back there with her apron on.

"Ms. Jackson."

She turned around with a grin. "You so silly. Come here."

I grabbed her in a bear hug, squeezing her until she squealed.

"Now, I see you got the apron on, but why don't I smell anything cooking?"

She stepped back and pointed to the counter, which was topped with an array of colorful vegetables in various stages of preparation.

"Savannah's got her heart set on gumbo," she announced. "Taurus wanted it, and you know that girl can't tell that boy, no."

"What's the problem with that?"

"You gotta stand over the roux 'til it's right. She ain't got time for that."

That was irritating to hear. The part about Savannah doing whatever my brother wanted her to do, that is. Not because I was jealous, but because it still pricked me sometimes to see him win. We'd always been competitive. It was a friendly rivalry, but that didn't make it any less significant.

I guess that's jealousy. I didn't wanna admit that.

"You need any help?" I said, just to be polite.

"Not from you," Mama retorted, making me laugh.

I could barely boil water.

"I'ma go holler at them for a minute."

She told me, "Go on," and commenced to chopping vegetables.

The guys were in the living room watching ESPN. When I plopped down on the couch next to Isaac, he handed me a beer.

"How's work?" he said.

"It's alright."

"You got a new project right?"

"Yeah. Aye, I need to be askin' *you* about work."

Isaac's chronically unemployed but finally working ass broke into a smile. "It's actually going good, man."

"T ain't actin' like an overseer?"

"Nah, I never see his ass."

Taurus nodded. "Cuz I'm the boss. I can't be rubbing shoulders with the proletariat."

"Fuck you." Isaac laughed. "He got me pushing paper, but it's a check. I ain't trying to go back in this time."

"That's what I like to hear. I'm proud of you." I looked at Taurus. "And you, too, man. You really stepped up."

He shrugged. "Wasn't shit. He got that job on his own."

"Yeah, speaking of, my probation officer is probably gonna call you soon," Isaac said. "Just to verify I'm still there."

"Bet." Taurus turned back to me. "You fucked ol' girl yet?"

Isaac's eyes got big behind his glasses. "You got a new one? What happened to the chick with all them kids?"

"That was Samara. Fizzled out. The last one was Jade."

Taurus pointed a finger at me. "You fucked her, didn't you?"

I shook my head. "Why you in my business? You got a baby, bout to get married, business going good. I don't understand it."

He smiled. "You just hate when I'm right."

"Which one are y'all talking about?" Isaac demanded. "I'm out the loop."

I sighed. "Alright. You were locked up back when I started working at Nexus."

"I remember. You got fired, right?"

"Nah. Not officially. Basically, me and this chick, Electra, got hired around the same time. She was bougie as fuck. Real stuck up. Nose in the air. Couldn't stand her ass."

Isaac smiled and exchanged a look with Taurus.

"Fuck you smilin' for, nigga?"

"Nothing. Keep going."

I eyed them before continuing my story. "Basically, we were working on this major project for a company called Evergreen. About six of us were on site for the project. Somebody accessed confidential company files from both of our computers. That's some serious shit. You can go to jail for that."

I smiled at Isaac. "Knowing you, you probably *already* been to jail for that."

Isaac held up his middle finger.

"Fast forward and we're back working together again."

"Hold up," Isaac said, scratching his beard. "What happened back then?"

I didn't like reliving it, but I went ahead and took him through it play by play.

Corporate espionage.

That was the accusation. That shit blindsided me.

We were both put on leave while they investigated. Shit was humiliating. A few weeks later, they told us they could find no concrete evidence of malicious intent to steal company information, but the damage was done at that point. We were both let go, our names tarnished in the industry. I blamed her. She blamed me and threatened to sue me. It got ugly.

"And that's why I been hustling and struggling with piddly shit for the past twelve years," I finished. "This StarTech shit is the first major project I've been on, and I ended up with her again. What are the fucking odds?"

"So she did that shit?"

I blew out a sigh. "I don't even know. She thinks I did it, I think she did it, but it lowkey wouldn't make sense for either one of us to do it and use our own computer. I've been thinking about that."

"Alright, alright." Taurus leaned forward with his elbows on his knees. "Did you fuck? That's all I wanna know."

"Yeah, nigga, damn. You happy now?"

He laughed. "As a matter of fact, I am. I should have bet money on that shit. That was, what, a week?"

"You the oldest and this is how you act."

"Shut the fuck up," he snapped. "What you even mad for? Pussy was trash?"

"Hell, nah. But that ain't the point."

"Then what's the point?"

"I still don't wanna work with her ass. And now, it's probably gon' be even worse. All tense and shit. Yall know me, I'm about my fucking business."

Taurus and Isaac both made the exact same face at the same time.

"So then...why'd you shit where you eat?"

I chuckled at the truth in Isaac's question. "It should be obvious, right? How many times have *y'all* turned down pussy from a beautiful woman?"

Very few straight men would count themselves in that number, my brothers least of all.

"Fair enough," Taurus conceded. "So when y'all start dating for real—"

"Whoa, whoa, slow down. Dead that shit right now. Ain't gon' be no dating. She still stuck up, and I still don't trust her ass."

Isaac elbowed me. "You ever thought about trying to figure out who was really behind that shit?"

"What's the point?"

"To clear your name," Taurus jumped in. "Then you wouldn't have to live and die by every little piddly project you get. Don't get me wrong, I respect the hustle, but that shit needs to pay off at some point."

My brothers had made a point worth considering, but I hadn't moved past the most important subject.

"She's fucking somebody else."

My brothers frowned at the same time.

"Who?" Isaac said.

"Electra. The one I just—my coworker."

"Why do you care?" Taurus said. "You just said you ain't datin' her and don't trust her."

"What makes you think I care?"

They looked at each other again, but this time, they both busted out laughing.

"Yall need to grow the fuck up."

The laughs got louder.

Taurus composed himself, his face going soft. "It's okay if you feelin' her, man."

I shook my head.

"The minute you said you couldn't stand her, I knew."

Taurus nodded at Isaac. "And I knew two weeks ago when you first told me about her."

"Knew what?"

"Yo ass always liked to tussle with these women, man. I never understood that shit," he said. "I like peace, but you be wantin' a challenge and shit. That's why you love your job so much, cuz you be havin' to argue and convince motherfuckers that you're worthy. It's all a game to you."

"Fuck outta here with that." I tilted my bottle up and swallowed several gulps of beer as I tried to pretend like he hadn't just clocked me.

"He ain't lyin'," Isaac chimed in with his equally unwanted opinion. "Yo cocky ass gets a thrill out of it. Always have."

"I don't know what y'all are talking about."

"Whatever, nigga. That's why you pussywhipped now."

Taurus laughed and mocked, "*She's fucking somebody else.*"

I look at him sideways. "You know, at this point, I think your newborn baby is more mature than you, nigga."

That just made them laugh harder.

Savannah poked her head out just then. "Hey, guys!"

"Hey, sis. You look good," I told her as I took in the sight of her glowing skin and healthy post-baby fullness.

"Thank you," she beamed. "Dinner in forty-five minutes."

We all nodded.

I looked over at Taurus just to see the look on his face. He always looked all dreamy and shit when she came around, and sure enough...that man had stars in his eyes.

"You need me to do anything?" he asked her.

She smiled and shook her head. "I'm fine."

"Yes, you are."

Her giggle followed her back into the kitchen, at which point Taurus leaned over and punched me on the shoulder.

"Don't be tellin' my wife she look good."

"Whatever. She does."

"Aye, T, how often do y'all drug test?"

Me and Taurus looked at our weed-smoking brother with the same expression—disbelief.

"I done told you a million times, it's random."

"You got a good job," I said. "Why you be so eager to fuck it up?"

Ignoring both of us, he said, "So if I smoked right now, today, what's the likelihood that I'd get tested in the next few days?"

Taurus shook his head. "I told you, I don't fucking know. You can't wait til you get back to your place?"

Of course he couldn't. He was hooked on that shit, as much as a person can be. But I wasn't judging today.

"Actually, I could smoke right now," I admitted. "I got some heavy shit on my mind."

"Alright. Let's walk."

Once we were far enough away from the house, Isaac lit up and we passed the blunt back and forth until we all felt giddy.

But leave it to me to bring down the mood.

"You know what I think about sometimes? Daddy. All the shit he got into trying to provide for us."

Taurus blew out a short sigh. "Failed at every last one."

"Exactly. You feel me. I don't wanna be that. I really don't."

"But I mean...you went to school," he said. "Did what you were supposed to do. You had a setback. That shit happens."

"Yeah, but I feel like I'm still crawling out of that fucking hole. And it ain't like I got a safety net out here."

"Who does? I worked my way up to where I am, man. So will you." He looked at Isaac. "And you. Maybe."

"And I admire you for that, but your story ain't my story, man."

Taurus shrugged like a man with a million dollars. "We write our stories, man. Get your fucking pen out and get to writing."

22

ELECTRA

First day back after…the incident.

If you can call mind-blowing sex and three orgasms an incident.

I felt like a new woman.

Lance had always been good enough, but Victor? Sex with him was what sex is supposed to feel like. I was convinced. But it was only one night, and we had reached the aftermath portion of the program. I was fine over the weekend when I was hiding out in my apartment, but now, in our office in the cold light of day, I was a ball of nerves.

"Good morning!"

"Morning, Nora." I watched her settle at her desk. "How was your weekend?"

She smiled. "It was wonderful. We took the kids to our cabin for the weekend. How was yours? Did you do anything interesting?"

"Why? Did you hear something?"

Her face tightened into a frown. "Um…no. Just making conversation."

"Sorry. I'm…" I trailed off, shaking my head. "My mind is all over the place. No, I just caught up on work."

She waved that away. "Girl, you need a social life. You don't go out?"

"I do. I actually have my father's birthday party coming up. Which I'm not looking forward to. But—"

I stopped abruptly when *he* walked in. It was probably my hormones talking, but he looked insanely good. He wore a simple black suit and a pink tie, but he looked fucking amazing in it.

I wanted him again.

Was that supposed to happen after hate sex?

That familiar ache settled between my legs, and I wondered how I was gonna get through the day.

Thankfully, his eyes avoided me completely. He greeted Nora like normal before passing me to get to his desk.

"How was your weekend, Victor?" she called out to him.

He looked back at Nora, his eyebrows up. "Why, what did you hear?"

I froze at his words, but Nora just shrugged and said, "Just making conversation," in her usual sing-song voice.

"I, uh, spent some time with the family," he answered, his voice low and cautious.

"How's the baby doing?"

"He's good. You know at that age, they mostly just lay there doing nothing. But he's good at it, I guess."

Nora chuckled. "Well, that's nice."

"Oh." Vic finally looked at me. "I was told to give you this."

He handed me a small blue envelope. In the process of taking it out of his hand, my finger brushed his. It was light enough to be an accident, but firm enough to send a bolt of electricity through me that was so strong, my body expelled a breath.

I wasn't going to make it through today.

And despite my intuition warning me not to, I raised my eyes to meet his. I knew what I'd find there, and I was correct: the slight dilation of his pupils and furrow of his brow contrasted with the softness in his expression, but they all worked together to communicate one unified emotion: longing.

My blood ran hot as I averted my eyes and snatched that envelope away, but it was too late. The heat was already spreading to all points south.

Heart pounding, I turned back to my work. The three of us worked in complete silence for over an hour, but my thoughts screamed at me, filling the lull with memories that should have had a triple-X sign flashing above them.

The man who sat no more than ten feet away from me had been inside me. He'd filled me up with several long, thick, hard inches and worked me until I came. He'd *tasted* me. I couldn't get past it. I still couldn't believe it.

And I wanted more.

"Okay, boys and girls, listen up!"

Nora's sudden announcement startled me. I turned in my chair to face her, careful not to look in his direction.

"Andrew emailed me. He's pleased with the results so far. He says keep it up."

I blew out a sigh of relief. "That's good news. Thank you, Nora."

"Thank *you*. Yall are making me look good out here."

On my way to turn back to my computer, I glanced over at him, but he didn't return the favor. That, too, was a relief. What happened earlier was just a fluke. The memories of him would fade with time, and nothing had to change here. He was right.

It was one night, and we never had to speak of it again.

I stared down at my buzzing phone.

> For such a hateful woman, you sound so sweet when you cum

My mouth dropped open. I immediately checked to see if Nora was looking at me, which she wasn't, and then I looked over at Victor. His back was to me, and he was typing away like nothing had happened.

I read it again just to make sure I hadn't imagined it, then I replied.

> That's highly inappropriate. Please don't text me like that again, especially at work. Behave yourself

Three bubbles appeared, and then:

> Make me

So childish. But if I responded, I'd fold. I knew that as sure as I knew my own name. So I put my phone on silent and tossed it into my tote.

A short time later, I heard rummaging sounds from his side of the office, then him murmuring, "Where the fuck is my pen?"

The more he rummaged, the bigger my smile grew. I'd forgotten all about my little Visconti caper. After the first day, I assumed he'd found it.

I turned around and watched him search, enjoying the sight of him bending, kneeling, foraging, and failing.

"Did you check your desk?" I finally said after I'd already watched him search his desk.

He turned around in a huff. "Obviously. Have you seen it?"

"What does it look like?"

"It's black and gold."

"BIC makes black and gold pens?"

"It's not a—look, have you seen it, or not?"

His frustration excited me, which signaled to me that I still couldn't stand him. What a relief.

"Maybe if you cleaned your desk, you'd be able to find things."

"Here, I'll help you look," Nora said, shooting me a disapproving glance as she passed by.

Victor checked his watch. "It's okay. It's here somewhere. You have that meeting, right?"

"Oh! Yes, I almost forgot. Thank you."

"No problem."

He watched her leave, then slowly brought his gaze down to me as the smile fell off his face. "I know you hid my pen."

I shook my head. "I don't know what you're talking about."

"You need to grow up. All this petty shit is unnecessary."

"Says the man who brought me ten pounds of almonds."

"Five. And that was different."

"Whatever."

"Where the fuck is my pen? That thing wasn't cheap."

"Then you should probably be more careful."

I was glad I was sitting when his intense stare took aim at my face. Weak in the knees doesn't describe the feeling that man conjured in me.

"Meet me in the parking garage in ten minutes."

That snapped me out of it. "For what?"

"We need to have a conversation."

"I have nothing to say to you."

"That's fine. Then you can listen."

I watched as he put his laptop on sleep mode and snatched his keys off his desk.

"I'm not meeting you," I said weakly.

He walked past me toward the door, calling out, "See you in ten," over his shoulder.

The nerve. The *gall*.

I stared after him, halfway expecting him to come back in and tell me he was joking. But after a few minutes passed, I realized he was serious, and I only had about five more minutes to shut down my computer and find his car in the garage.

23

Vic

"Took you long enough."

Thirteen minutes after my directive, Electra slid into the passenger seat of my car in a huff.

"I almost didn't come," she said.

"Now why don't I believe that?"

She looked around nervously. "Because this is reckless."

"And yet, here you are."

"Basic service call," she said. "Don't get excited."

"I kinda need to be excited to service you properly, so..."

She rolled her eyes. "You *are* gonna drive to a secluded spot, right?"

"Yes, Electra. Despite my lowly Howard education, I'm smart enough to know not to fuck you where somebody can see. Come on, Harvard."

"Penn."

"I do not give a *fuck*."

"Still insecure, I fear."

"You need to fear this dick."

She burst out laughing as I cranked up the car.

"Am I funny, Electra? How the fuck am I funny? I'm here to fuckin' amuse you?"

To my surprise, homegirl laughed harder, passing the vibe check with flying colors.

"I can't believe you of all people saw *Goodfellas*," I said as I waited for her to put on her seatbelt.

"Who hasn't?"

"Again, my answer would have been you."

"Whatever, Victor."

Once her belt was clicked into place, I drove around until I reached the top of the parking deck. A lone silver Mercedes sat at the top, no doubt somebody's precious baby, too pretty to risk being hit by someone else's door. I parked on the far side of the deck, furthest away from the stairs and elevator.

I checked the locks, then turned the radio down. No music for her. Just dick.

"Why'd you hide my pen?" I said as I unbuckled my pants. "Shit was petty."

"Why are you so sure I hid it?" She lifted her hips, pushing her stockings down and stepping out of them. "Maybe Nora borrowed it and put it back in the wrong spot."

"See, this is why I don't trust you." I grabbed my wallet out of my back pocket and pulled out a rubber. "Just be honest about it. I might even respect you for it."

She pushed her panties down, then held them up for me to see. My dick swelled and sprang to life as I watched the lacy red thong swing back and forth at the end of her pinky finger like a hypnotist's pocket watch.

"What would make you think I care about having your respect?" she asked.

I didn't bother to answer. I was too busy snatching her panties off her finger and tucking them into the side pocket of my jacket. Her eyes followed my fingers as they reached into my pants and widened as my dick popped out. I rolled the condom on, wondering if she'd ever put it in her mouth. That's not really something you do for a man when you hate him, but I never really knew with her. She'd already shocked me once. The fact that she was about to fuck me in my car was still surreal to me. *And* she let me have her panties.

No time to worry about that, though.

I looked over at her and inclined my head to the left to call her to me. I slid my seat back, then reclined it. She climbed right on, but she hovered over me.

"What's the problem?"

She sighed. "I did hide your pen."

"I know that." My hands went to her hips and found warm, silky skin there. "What you waitin' on? Sit on that motherfucker."

"Why do you have to be so vulgar all the time?"

"It ain't all the time, it's when I'm turned on. Sit yo fine ass down, Electra."

"*Okay.*" She lowered herself onto me, and we both exhaled at the same damn time.

An inferno surrounded me as she sank down and fully seated herself. I struggled to keep my eyes open. My entire body pulsed with pleasure, but even excluding the sexual act, it felt so damn good to relax and enjoy something. The tension left me. All the shit I was worried about was gone. All that was left was this, and *this* was the best pussy I'd ever had. And it wasn't even close.

I knew it good because I felt it even with a condom on. Condom sex was always mediocre for me. Necessary, but mid. I could always cum, but it was usually a long journey to get there. But this right here was something different. And I was telling the truth when I told her I never would have thought she was holding something like this.

The inside of a car wasn't the best place for this, but she was also pretty damn good at riding me in spite of the limitations. Up and down, she floated on my dick. Her body felt weightless, but that pussy was fat. Had my teeth gritting.

With her leaned over me, I had a perfect view down the front of her shirt. Nice-sized titties greeted me, as did a gold necklace with a cross on it.

Lord forgive me.

I wanted to touch. I wanted to lick and suck. But that wasn't the kind of sex we were having, so I busied myself with watching her, which was just as arousing. As hard as she was working to hold back and not react, she was real easy to read in the light of day. Her tense face, heavy breathing, rolling eyes, and fingernails digging into my shoulders let me know how much she liked my dick.

We didn't agree on much, but we damn sure had some common ground here.

"*Fuck.*" I didn't mean to let that come out. Trying to beat her at her own game, I guess, but shit. What else do you do when it feels this good?

"You like that?"

I opened my eyes and lifted my head from the headrest, unaware of how I even got there. I was completely alert a minute ago. "You talking to me?"

Her eyes narrowed. "Yeah. Do you like it?"

She was so wet. Tight, too. Pussy clamping down on my dick like a fucking vice I didn't wanna escape from.

"Hell, yeah I like it." I stared at her eyes, at the golden brown flecks that seemed like they were sparkling in the light of the sun. Every thing about this woman was pretty. Even the tiny moles that scattered across her neck like the stars did across the sky.

"Mmmm."

Finally. I almost smiled at the sound of her little moan. I'd told her she sounded sweet, and that was true, but more than anything else, she was impossibly sexy. My dick twitched inside her. I know she felt it. I hoped she did.

Not that it mattered.

In a fit of...something, I leaned in to kiss her. Just before my lips reached hers, she opened her eyes, and then this woman raised her hand and mushed my fucking face.

"What the fuck?" I demanded. It didn't hurt, but it stung.

She stilled her body. "Don't kiss me."

"It was a reflex. You ain't have to get violent."

"Sorry. But why would you—"

"Because you look beautiful with my dick inside you." I let my head fall back against the headrest. "I got carried away."

She took a deep breath. "That's the only time I look beautiful?"

I reached up and put my hand on the back of her head, grabbing a handful of her hair. "You look beautiful every fucking time I look at you. That's why I'm always looking."

Her face softened into something that was almost in the ball park of a smile. And since she was even more beautiful when she smiled, I knew I had to end that.

"Enough talking. Ride this shit, girl."

When she moved again, it looked and felt like something possessed her. Her mouth went slack, her full lips parting until a little 'o' formed between them. I stared at them, knowing they were soft, wishing I could prove myself right before reminding myself we didn't do that. *Couldn't* do that. Because that's what you do when there are feelings. We didn't have those, unless you counted hate.

I stared down at the place where our bodies met. Like a key in a lock, we fit. I felt myself getting close to blastoff with every creamy roll of her hips. My head fell back, my eyes drifted shut, and my teeth sank into my bottom lip as low groans rumbled in my throat.

Then something strange happened.

My shirt lifted and two hands slid under it, coming to rest on my chest. She was *touching* me.

Two palms. That's it. That's all. They shouldn't have affected me the way they did, but something about her soft touch had me spinning. My hand, still in her hair, balled into a fist, and I gave a slight tug before pulling with force. She gasped just before her eyes rolled back, and I realized I'd just learned something about her.

I couldn't wait to pull it from the back.

My other hand went to her ass, gripping a little too hard with absolutely no apologies. Other than a tiny flinch, she didn't seem to mind.

"Yessss..." she moaned.

That set me off.

I pistoned my hips, stroking her from the bottom, bouncing her on me. Her moans got louder; my groans turned to animalistic grunts.

"Hold up," I gritted out, but she kept going, bouncing and rolling while I fought that nut with everything I had.

A few seconds later, I was unsuccessful, but damn if it didn't feel good to lose. I threw my head back and busted. It was intense, just like I told her before the first time we did this. Long and strong, that nut had me in a chokehold for a good minute. I tasted blood in my mouth. Must have bit my tongue.

It was worth it.

"Why didn't you stop?" I asked her, my eyes still closed. My body jerked when she ran her hands down my chest and across my abs.

"I wanted you to cum."

"I was gon' cum regardless," I said, opening my eyes. "I wanted you to get yours first."

She stared at me without blinking. "Lunch isn't over."

"True, indeed." I took a deep breath, waiting for my heartbeat to slow.

I brought my hand around and slid it between us as she lifted off of me, allowing my dick to fall limply back in its place. I slid two fingers inside her, happy to have the chance to please her with a clear head. I could concentrate on her, now. I could learn more.

With my fingers, I got lost in the sauce, stroking her while she rolled her hips again, chasing the pleasure. With my thumb, I strummed her clit like a guitar, playing a tune we would both learn by heart if I had my way.

"Oh, God, yes..." she bucked against my fingers, her head falling forward. I cocked my head to the side like a dog, trying to learn her language. With enough practice, I would figure out exactly what she liked. Maybe I'd even teach her something new. Time would tell.

"No rush, but are you close?"

"Sounds like you're rushing me," she breathed.

"Not at all. Just curious."

"I am."

I figured. With that knowledge, I curved my fingers, massaging the hard lump I'd found deep inside her. With my other hand, I pulled her hair harder, pleased with the sound she made when I did it.

"Yeah," I said. "You like that."

She didn't respond.

My eyes narrowed. "I know your instinct is to fight me, but when we're doing this, don't pretend like you don't enjoy it." I loosened my fist and used my fingers to massage her head. She seemed to like a little roughness, but she also deserved soft caresses. I delivered them on her scalp. And on her clit. The stimulation was taking her there, I could feel it in the way her walls tightened. In the way her pussy lubricated itself. So hot and slippery. My dick rocked up again.

I bit my lip. She was so fucking sexy like this, with her brows knitted together, eyes rolled back, bottom lip between her teeth. I could barely stand to look at her.

She grabbed my hand, pulled it off the back of her head, and locked her eyes on mine as she brought my hand to her face and sucked my middle finger into her mouth.

"Fuck." My face formed into a grimace while I watched her fellate my finger. That shit came out of nowhere. Pleasant fucking surprise right there.

Her eyes fell to my dick, which was back at full attention. She grabbed the tip of the condom and pulled, making a mess in my lap as my nut dripped out. She tossed it aside and grabbed my dick. With my fingers in her pussy and in her mouth, she used hers to jack me off.

It was kinda chaotic, but in a good way.

"Damn, girl. What got into you?"

She smiled around my finger. "You did."

I watched helplessly as she licked it, then sucked it back into her mouth.

"Hold up." I pulled my fingers out of her and held them up as an offering. "Might as well taste yourself since you doin' all that."

With no hesitation, she switched hands, licking her cream off my other fingers before sucking them into her mouth.

"Tastes good, don't it?" I asked, quiet and strained. She was still jacking me off, bringing me right back to the edge. I was balancing precariously, fully aware that it wouldn't take much to push me over.

I reclaimed possession of my hand, bringing it back to her center to finish the job. It didn't take long, either. Her hand stuttered on my dick as she came with a loud wail. I was right behind her, spurting into her fist as she milked me until I was fully drained of every last drop.

Back to back.

This woman was something special.

"Shit." I was tired as fuck. Apparently, she was, too. She leaned forward and rested her body against mine, her head tucked into my neck.

Her body felt good flush against me. We fit there, too. Comfortable. But before I could bring my hands to rest on her back, she sat up and climbed off of me, landing back in her seat on the passenger side.

The only sounds were our labored breaths and the patter of the first raindrops out of the gray sky. Electra stared straight ahead, her eyes unfocused. I stretched my hand out and grabbed the hem of her skirt, tugging it down until it covered her thighs. Her eyes shifted to me then, and I met her gaze with my own. A chill went down my spine. Something like electricity coursed through my veins.

The discomfort from those sensations made me drop my eyes. I noticed her pearl necklace was upside down. I reached out and rotated it with my fingers until the clasp was hidden behind her. With that, I felt like I'd done my part to put her back together again.

"We should get back," I said. "Lunch is over."

"Just a second."

I looked over at her again, waiting to hear what she had to say, but it turned out to be absolutely nothing, except, "Okay, now we can go."

I shook my head, but I couldn't help but be amused by her. Always fighting. Always...tussling.

My brothers' words flashed in my mind.

I started my car and began the slow drive back to reality. "Can I ask you something?"

"I suppose."

"What were you listening to the other day when I came in the office?"

"What day?"

"The day I came in late. The day we fucked for the first time."

She hesitated before saying, "Just my R&B playlist."

"You like R&B?"

"I love R&B. But, who doesn't?" She was quiet for a moment. "It was SiR. He's amazing."

I filed that away.

Back in the office, she reached into my drawer and retrieved my pen, smirking as she handed it over.

I tucked it in my suit jacket pocket, right next to her panties.

24

ELECTRA

QADIR STOPPED ME ON my way to the elevators. I was so startled, I almost dropped my Starbucks.

"I am so sorry!" He grabbed my bag, which was rapidly sliding down my shoulder. "You okay?"

"I'm fine. And good morning to you."

"Morning. I wanted to ask you something."

"Can you talk and walk? I'm running late."

"Of course." His long strides easily kept pace with me. "Can we grab lunch some time?"

"Um, yes. That would be fine."

I don't know why I agreed. Qadir was attractive, but I already had Lance in my life, and...whatever this was with Machiavelli. Adding a third man to this already odd state of affairs was asking for trouble.

"Should we schedule, or should I just come by and scoop you?"

I laughed at that. "You can just come by."

He smiled down at me. His brand of handsome wasn't like Victor's. Qadir had soft features. "Then I most certainly will." We stopped at the door to my office. "Have a good day, beautiful."

"You, too."

I watched him leave, then walked in and came face to face with the judge and jury that was Nora's disapproving face.

"Morning," I said pointedly.

She shook her head. "Morning to you, too."

"What?"

"I ain't sayin' a word."

She didn't have to say it, though. I already knew. And I'll admit, there is a part of me, way deep down, that likes mess. *Was*, I mean. I'd left that behind. At least, I thought I had.

I sat down and got right to work. There was much to do today; we had a major milestone coming up, and you do not want to miss those. It's basically career suicide.

Victor strolled in and spoke to Nora before passing me with a bored, "Good morning."

"Hey."

I allowed myself one minute to reminisce about the other day in his car, and then I refocused on the task at hand. I'd already lost hours reliving it over the last few days. Somehow, the second time was even better than the first. Riding him in his car on my lunch break under the threat of discovery was the perfect storm of hedonism.

That night, and not for long, I let myself imagine what it might be like to let hate sex grow into something more. It was difficult to see, blurry like a bad photo, but the possibility of it was enough to satisfy me.

Then I came to my senses.

Outside of sex, the man was a virus.

"What the fuck?"

I whirled around and saw Victor stooped over in front of his laptop.

"What's wrong?"

"What the hell is this?" he bellowed.

I jumped up and approached him cautiously.

"What happened?"

"Stan Cromer just sent us an email about the strategic plan. He said he has a few notes, but overall, it looks good."

My head swam at that news. "But it wasn't supposed to go out until Friday."

"Exactly!" His eyes narrowed. "Two days was too long for you to wait?"

"Me?"

"Who else? Unbelievable."

"Wait, why would I send out something we hadn't agreed on yet?"

His irate stare wounded me. "For the same reason you do anything, Electra. So you can be the best. Or the first. Glory hogging is a sport with you at this point. I don't know what the f—" he stopped abruptly, his eyes shifting to Nora. "I don't know why I thought anything would be different this time."

Nora walked up behind me. "Wait a minute—"

"I didn't send shit, Victor! The last correspondence I had about the plan was when I sent my part to you and Nora for your approval."

My heart pounded. "Why am I explaining myself to you? For all I know, *you* did this and you're trying to flip it on me."

"Guys—"

"Just when I think you changed, you go and remind me," he said. "You still the same shady—"

"Enough!" Nora walked around me and stood between us. "This has gone on long enough."

She took a deep breath. "Look. I didn't realize it, but *I* sent out the draft by mistake."

Victor and I both looked at her. "You did?" I said.

"Yes. I just got the email myself. I was gonna tell you. I sent you my feedback, which wasn't much. I was putting together the list of emails to send to you to make sure you sent it out to the right people and somehow, I ended up forwarding it to them as well. I apologize."

Victor blew out a sigh. "This is not good."

"It's not, but it's fixable."

"Well, this Stan person said he only had a few notes," I said. "That's promising, I guess."

Nora reached out and touched my shoulder. "Please accept my apology."

The sincerity in her eyes was clear. Her explanation didn't make total sense to me, but from the start, she'd struck me as someone who wasn't very technologically savvy.

"It's okay, Nora. It happens."

"Yeah," Vic said. "No worries."

She nodded. "I'll work on fixing my mistake. But you two? That's a much bigger task."

"What do you mean?"

Her eyes darted back and forth between the two of us. "Do y'all know I have to send a status report once a week?"

Vic nodded. "That's standard."

"Did you know there's a section on professionalism?"

He and I exchanged a glance.

"This? Is a problem," she announced. "Now, I want y'all to win, so I've kept all this foolishness out of my reports."

"I appreciate that."

"Thank you."

He and I spoke those words at the same time.

"You're welcome. But enough is enough. My job is to answer your questions and give you advice from StarTech's perspective. So here it is: y'all don't trust each other. I know you have history, God only knows what it is, but you're letting it wreck your professional chemistry. Which is pretty darn good, from what I've seen. You two," she pointed a finger at Victor, then at me, "need to get it together. Today."

Our eyes locked again before we looked away.

"Do you need a mediator?"

"We're fine," I told her. "It was a misunderstanding, that's all."

"I agree." Victor put on a tight smile that didn't reach his eyes. "Sorry, Electra. I shouldn't have accused you."

Through gritted teeth, I responded, "I appreciate that. And I shouldn't have raised my voice."

A few silent seconds passed before he said, "Great. Back to work."

"Yep," I said. "Lots to do."

Nora shook her head. "Nice try. Nope, we're not letting this fester anymore. Give me a day."

The next day, Nora revealed her grand reconciliation plan.

"Trust exercises? The fuck is this shit?"

I chuckled at that. She'd placed the packet of stapled papers on the conference table before she headed off to her meeting, announcing that we had until the end of the day to complete at least two of the exercises and report on the outcome.

The consequence of inaction? She was going to report what happened yesterday.

I didn't buy that at all, but I was also a little scared to get on her bad side, so here we were, sitting in our chairs across from each other, trying to figure out which exercises to complete.

"Let me see," I said, holding out my hand. I suppose she only gave us one packet so that we'd have to work together.

Ugh.

"There's no way in hell I'm letting you blindfold me," I said, mentally nixing the first three exercises.

"I thought the same thing," he said. "Might end up face down with a knife in my back."

"Whatever. And I'm not falling around you."

"I'd catch you, but that's just cuz I'm a gentleman. Ain't got shit to do with trust."

"That gentleman thing? I have yet to see that in action, but okay."

He sat in silence while I skimmed the rest of the list. Team building puzzle. Role reversal. Two truths and a lie. Team juggling. Shared vision board.

Corporate culture is so lame.

"What about the commonality game?"

He held out his hand. After reading the instructions, he shrugged. "This one's cool." He read the next page. "Compliment circle. That'll be the second one. All we gotta do is talk to each other."

"Why don't we just get back to work and *say* we did these?"

He had the nerve to look disappointed. "Your lack of integrity continues to confound me."

My eyes narrowed, but I let that pass. Could have been teasing. I couldn't read all of his vibes yet. "What are the rules for the first game?"

"We set a timer for five minutes. In that time, we have to come up with as many commonalities as we can."

"Fine," I said. "Use your phone."

"And you keep score."

I reached back and grabbed my pen and notepad. "I'm ready."

He set the timer, propped his phone, and we were off.

"My favorite food is pizza."

I rolled my eyes. "That's how you start? You're so basic. Mine's lobster."

"Lobster's not a meal, it's a crustacean."

I pouted. "Lobster fra diavolo, then."

"Better. Your turn."

I sighed. This was so stupid.

"You already know this, but I love R&B."

"Me, too. Jot that."

"I *am*. Go."

"I love dogs, but I don't have one."

"Me, too." I made another tally mark. "Um…I love baby pink tea roses."

He stared blankly. "What I look like?"

"Whatever. This is dumb."

"Yes, it is." He glanced at his phone. "Four more minutes. Damn."

"It's your turn."

He blew out a sigh. "Alright. Shit. Um…I want kids eventually."

"Same." I marked the paper. "I love true crime."

"I don't, but that tracks."

I rolled my eyes.

"I think Marvel is better than DC, but they both fell off."

I chuckled. "I actually agree with that." Another mark. "I'm religious but I don't go to church."

He nodded. "Yeah. Same."

We had enough for the gate line. I drew it and waited.

His eyes narrowed, then flickered over me, lingering on my legs. Per usual. "I got one."

I raised my eyebrows.

"I'm attracted to my coworker."

I averted my eyes, but the damage had already been done with his words. I stared down at the paper and wordlessly drew a sixth line.

He chuckled, then silence followed.

"How much more time?" I asked quietly.

Before he could answer, his phone began to buzz, signaling the end of our misery. This round, anyway. I cleared my throat and tore the page out of the notebook to provide to Nora as evidence that we completed the task.

One down.
One to go.

25

Vic

"For this one, we're just supposed to alternate giving each other compliments," she explained. She was giving off a sexy teacher vibe. Or maybe I was just horny again. Seemed constant ever since our first time.

"That seems easy enough," I said.

"Does it?"

"All the lies you tell yourself about how amazing you are, just tell 'em to me instead."

She rolled her eyes for probably the fiftieth time today. "Do we need a timer for this one?"

"No, but I'ma set it anyway. No need to waste any more time than we have to."

"Agreed."

I reset the timer and pressed the button. "I'll start. Now, don't let this go to your head, but you're extremely intelligent."

Her face lit up for a nanosecond before she composed herself. "Thanks. Don't sound so surprised."

"I didn't sound surprised, Electra."

"You did, but it's okay. Um, well, I guess I'd have to say I admire your ability to occasionally say nice things and actually sound sincere."

I frowned at that. "What the fuck does that mean?"

"Charm," she said like it had been on the tip of her tongue. "You're very charming."

"Thanks, I guess." I waited. "Is it my turn?"

"Uh, *yeah*."

"That. Right there. I truly admire how expressive your voice can be. You wield it like an instrument. Different pitches and whatnot. Like just a second ago, you successfully conveyed your extreme annoyance. Well done."

Her eyes flashed. "Wow. Well, you have the uncanny ability to make your insults sound almost...poetic."

I nodded. "Okay, here's a genuine compliment. You're a beautiful woman."

"Thank you. And you're..." she trailed off, allowing herself a minute to study me. "You're handsome, I guess."

I laughed. "You really had to dig deep for that one, huh?"

"No, that's how I feel. I just...didn't wanna say it, I guess."

"I get that."

We let that pass.

I glanced at my phone. Three minutes and forty-eight seconds remained of this little circle jerk. I figured I might as well make this shit interesting.

"I admire your professionalism."

She lowkey beamed at that, which I knew she would.

"What I mean is that it amazes me that you come in here every day and act like I don't know how you taste."

Her face fell, then twisted into a scowl. I saw that coming, too.

"What you mad for?" I teased. "You taste good."

"I thought we agreed to keep that out of the office." She'd lowered her voice like there was someone here to overhear.

"Did we?"

Her lips formed a tight line, then a resolve seemed to come over her. She relaxed in her seat.

"Everything is a game to you," she finally said.

"What makes you say that?"

She shook her head. "Anyway, it's my turn. You're extremely proficient at making me cum, and I truly appreciate that."

I swallowed hard as my blood started rushing to its favorite gathering spot of late. I shifted in my seat and made a pitiful attempt to cross my legs before she saw my erection, but it was too late. And her smirk indicated that was the whole fucking point.

Fine.

If she wanted to play, we could play.

"Am I extremely proficient, or are you so attracted to me, you can't help it?"

"That's not a compliment, Victor."

This fucking woman.

"Fine. You're one of the sexiest women I've ever met in my entire life."

She crossed her legs, mirroring me. "Oh, really?"

"Yeah."

"Well...you're also very sexy."

"I know."

She chuckled. "Your confidence level is astonishing."

I glanced at the door. Nora had closed it behind her when she left.

"I love how passionate you are," I said. "I never expected it."

"And I appreciate how skilled you are at...eating..."

I uncrossed my legs and leaned forward, resting my elbows on my knees. "Eating what, Electra?"

She shrugged a shoulder.

"You can say it. I want you to say it to me."

The fire in her gaze intensified. "You already know."

I decided to have mercy on her this time, much as I wanted to hear it and watch it come out of her pretty lips.

"Your turn," she breathed.

"I appreciate how wet you get for me."

I saw the moment that one hit. Taurus once told me it's easier to get in a woman's bed than it is to get in her head. I never forgot that, and at this moment, I felt like a pro.

"I have more than a passing appreciation for the size of your penis," she finally retorted. "And the way you use it."

I laughed at the formality. It felt like her way of keeping me at a distance.

"I derive immense satisfaction from the fact that you hate me, but you still care about my enjoyment. And I know this because I feel you squeeze your walls when I'm inside you."

She took a deep breath.

"Not that you need to. That little pussy is tight as fuck."

She stared down at the floor beneath her. "I said you were handsome. It's true, but also...you're *gorgeous*. And I never say that about men. Your face..." she brought her eyes back up to mine. "All I can think about is how much I want to sit on it."

"I like the fact that you're being honest now. I hope you keep that up. Like I told you, I'm here to serve."

We stared at each other for a moment before I reminded her, "It's your turn."

Her lips parted, but just before she spoke, my phone buzzed. I almost knocked it off the table when I moved to silence it, but she didn't seem to notice. She looked like she was in a daze.

"Seems like we're done," I said. "But we can keep going."

"I think we should probably stop."

"Should we?"

She nodded. "Are you still hard?"

I sat back to give her the full picture, which was my dick giving her a salute, making a tent in my slacks.

"Are you still wet?"

She crossed her arms in front of her. "I never said I was wet."

"You don't have to."

The corners of her mouth twitched, but she fought that smile as hard as she was fighting me.

"It appears we may have a different problem on our hands now," she said.

"We don't need Nora to fix this one, though."

She laughed at that. "I don't know. The way you flirt with her—"

"That's charm, remember?"

"Whatever." Her smile lingered. "I guess we can tell her our mission was a success."

"Yeah. I have one more compliment, though."

"What?"

"I appreciate that you're letting me see that soft side of you now."

She killed her smile. "That was an accident, I assure you."

"Oh, I bet it was," I agreed. "But I like it."

Her eyes dropped as a wave of shyness seemed to overtake her. "I told you, it comes out when people do things to deserve it."

"Mmm."

The door swung open, and in walked Nora with a grin on her face.

I whirled around in my chair and slid over to my desk. Electra hopped up and hurried over to Nora. "We finished!"

"How'd it go?"

"It went well. Here's the proof. We did two exercises, and—"

"Girl, I don't need to see that. I just need to know y'all did what needed to be done."

I adjusted myself, smiling to myself at her words.

I worked out extra hard at the gym tonight. I had energy to burn and nobody to burn it on. All that foreplay actually drove me up a weight level.

I was cooling down when I saw a familiar face headed toward me.

"K!"

"Vic!"

Kelvin Macarther strolled toward me with a huge grin on his face. The last few years had put a little weight on him, but he looked the same otherwise.

We dapped and hugged. "What's up, bruh?" he said. "What you been doin' with yourself?"

"Shit, grindin'."

"I feel you. Where you working right now?"

I stood a little taller. "I got my own thing, man. On my own."

"That's what's up."

"What about you?"

He sneered. "I'm still with PMG."

"Don't do that," I laughed. "You ain't liking it?"

"It's a check."

We shared a laugh at that. It was a big check, I was sure. PMG was one of the big five firms. That probably would have been my destination if not for what happened at Nexus.

"Just out of curiosity, what's the market looking like out there for consultants?"

His face fell. "You, uh, you looking to make a move?"

"I think so. This solo shit is too sometimey."

"You're so talented," he said. "You sure you wanna give up your autonomy? I mean, my check is nice, but I'm a cog in the machine. Which suits me, to be fair. But you've always been more creative. You know what I mean?"

"Yeah. I hear you. It's just not going the way I thought it would, that's all."

"Stick with it, Vic. It'll pay off eventually."

"I notice you ain't answer my question, though."

He chuckled, putting his hands up in surrender. "You got me."

"I know. What's the deal?"

He sighed. "Alright. Here's the real. Your name still got that Nexus shit attached to it. You know how the industry is, man. People talk. They're still talking."

"Twelve fucking years."

I said this like I didn't already know the deal. I'd heard the whispers before. Every time I showed up to pitch. Every time a big client let me down easy. In the break rooms of my small clients. I was damaged goods out here.

"I appreciate you for being real with me." I stuck out my hand.

He gave me a shake. "You good, though?"

"Yeah. I'm on a major project. I'm just not sure how it's gonna shake out, that's all."

"You got this, man. And I'm here if you ever need to talk. This business ain't for the weak."

Ten minutes later, I sat in my car thinking about the state of affairs. StarTech wasn't gonna last forever, and even if things went perfectly from here on out, my name was still tarnished. Honestly, I was lucky—*we* were lucky to even get that account.

Frustrated, I picked up my phone.

> Can I see you tonight?

I have plans

> Lance?

> If you must know…yes

>> Fuck him

>> Actually, don't fuck him.

>> You know what I mean

> LOL

This shit was upsetting. I wanted to take all my anger out on her pussy tonight, and she wouldn't cooperate. But I couldn't even be mad at her. Hate fucking only satisfies one part of you. It doesn't do a thing for the rest of your needs.

>> Enjoy your date

> Thank you, I will. Enjoy your hand

I couldn't do anything but twist my lips and shake my head at that shit. Well played, Medusa.

And the sad part was, I was actually gonna do it.

Her panties were tucked neatly and discreetly in the bottom drawer of my closet island. I pulled them out and set them on my bathroom counter.

After my shower, I took them to bed with me. I pictured her face while I jacked my dick with those red lace panties wrapped around my hand. It wasn't quite as good as the real thing, but it was good enough to satisfy me.

For about ten minutes.

It kept me from thinking about her date.

For about ten minutes.

I wasn't worried about him, though.

I was worried about her.

Lance had to be a letdown after fucking with me.

26

ELECTRA

THE CLOSER IT GOT to my father's birthday extravaganza, the more anxious I became.

My brother's anniversary was manageable because it was a carefully regimented program. The birthday party would be something else entirely. It would be a social event with the requisite social rules, but more importantly, it would be open season on me and all my flaws.

Nora noticed my discontent when I arrived at the office. She badgered me and badgered me until she wore me down. I waited until Victor, who'd been quiet, left the office on a break to tell her.

"So what's the issue, dear?" she said.

"It's gonna be…it's hard to explain. Do you have a family member who's the golden child?"

Nora shook her head.

"Well, in my family, it's my brother. It's always stressful being around him with the rest of my family. He's okay on his own, but when my parents are there? It's nonstop shade and passive aggressive nonsense."

"Don't go," was her simple answer.

I gave a sad smile. "I have to. It's my father's sixtieth birthday."

"Got it. You can't miss that." She stared at me over the top of her reading glasses. "How old are you, sweetheart?"

"Thirty-six."

"You're old enough to tell them where to go and how to get there, I would think." She paused to take a sip of tea. "I was forty when I realized that as much as I loved my parents, I didn't owe them a damn thing."

"It's different in my family. I owe them a lot, and expectations are high."

"Is it intimate, or will there be lots of people there?"

I rolled my eyes. "Dr. Joss Montrose is being feted in the grand ballroom at Summerville's City Hall."

"Oh. Okay, then, Dr. Is it black tie?"

"Semi-formal. My father hates all that fussiness."

"Well, can you at least take a friend? Have somebody there with you to give you some moral support?"

I'd already asked Ciara. Unfortunately for me, my best friend had a better offer in the form of a six foot two magistrate judge named Sterling. I didn't expect or want her to pass that up just to babysit me.

Victor returned just then, passing us to settle at his desk.

"I'll be fine," I said to end the conversation, punctuating my statement with a firm head nod.

"Hey, Victor?"

"Yes, Ms. Nora."

She giggled in that silly way she always did when Victor was doing his charming routine. He'd only said her name, but I had to admit, the man had the kind of voice that would sound sexy reading the Declaration of Independence. And the way he looked at you when you had his attention made you feel like the only girl in the world. I shivered thinking about it.

"What are you doing this weekend?"

I cut my eyes at her, but she didn't notice.

He turned in his chair to face us. "I'm not sure yet. I'll be outside, though. It's supposed to be beautiful."

"Hot date?" she asked with a grin.

"Why, you tryna roll? I done told you about that, Nora. Your husband ain't gon' like it."

Her giggle was as exaggerated as my eye roll.

"Actually, me and Electra were just talking about a birthday party she's going to that probably won't be all that fun for her."

His eyes moved back and forth between me and Nora. "Why is that?"

"Family messiness," Nora answered at the same time I said, "It doesn't matter."

His eyes settled on me. "You should take Larry."

"It's Lance," I said, but he had already turned back to his work.

Nora batted her eyelashes at me a few times before returning to her seat, and I stood there bewildered, wondering what she was trying to accomplish with her meddling.

She'd questioned me about what she perceived as feelings between me and Victor. Then she called us out on our trust issues and made us remedy that. Now, she seemed to be trying to play matchmaker. And frankly, that wasn't her job. I'd been letting it slide, but maybe it was time to nip it in the bud, along with whatever this was with Victor. Clearly we weren't as good at hiding it as we thought we were.

My job was way more important than sex. Even good sex. Well, amazing sex. The best sex I'd ever had. The waters were getting murky here, and that made me uncomfortable, especially with the party looming.

Focus was the name of the game.

27

Vic

ANOTHER FRIDAY NIGHT AT home alone.

It was cool, though. I had work to catch up on. We were nearing the midpoint in the project, and another milestone was approaching.

But sitting in my office and staring out the window wasn't doing anything to foster my productivity. My mind was heavy, full of thoughts of the future.

And the past.

Because those two periods were inextricably linked and working together to complicate my present.

I shared some of the blame, though. It was my worries about the future that were the real problem. I knew that, and yet I still couldn't manage to live in the moment, taking each day as it came. There were too many milestones in my own life that I wanted to hit.

How was I supposed to take care of a family without stability in my career? I've never run from pressure, but this felt like more than that. I was restless. Anxious. Under the gun. But for what, though? I didn't even have a date, much less a wifely prospect.

I'm trippin'.

My father crossed my mind just then. He usually did when I wallowed in self-pity.

He was a good man in a lot of ways, but he dropped the ball where it counted. There was no way in hell I'd ever put my family through all the bullshit he inflicted on us with his irresponsibility.

Lights cut off. Foreclosure notices. Car repossessed. Utilities and bills put in our names before we were even out of middle school. I was miles away from that now, but instability, any at all, was out of the question for my family. My *future* family.

I wasn't getting shit done any time soon, so I picked up my phone and dialed someone from my past.

"O'neal!"

He was quiet for a moment, probably trying to place my voice. Then, "Victor? Damn! How long's it been?"

"It's been a minute."

"It has. What you been up to?"

"I'm out on my own now."

"Oh, word? Good for you."

"You still consulting?"

His sarcastic laugh was all the answer I needed. "Nah, I'm managing a startup now."

"Look at you! That's what's up."

"Yeah, man. I couldn't stay in that rat race. Shit'll kill you."

"You ain't lyin'. Listen, I wanna pick your brain about something."

"What's up?"

"You heard from any of our Nexus cohort?"

"Nah, man. Not in a few years."

That didn't surprise me. We were all from different places geographically, but we shared a few very important similarities. Namely, that none of us were white males. We came in as part of a diversity initiative, and we were the best and the brightest. Funny how half of us were now on our own.

"I got to thinking on what happened," I said. "With the investigation and all."

"Yeah. That was some foul shit."

"Yeah. It's still following me."

"I'm not surprised. I heard Mario owns a few restaurant franchises. I saw Melanie about three years ago at a Cowboys game. She got married, had kids. I wanna say she don't even work anymore."

"What about Xiang?"
"Oh, yeah. You were already gone when Xiang left."
"She quit?"
"Yeah. About a month after y'all got let go. They were on some shady shit with her. They hired a translator—"
"Xiang spoke English."
"Exactly. They said they couldn't understand her. That kinda shit, man. After a while, it got to be too much, and she just left."
"Damn."
"I ain't seen or heard from Electra since, though."
I smiled to myself. He didn't need to worry about Electra.
We chatted a few minutes longer before I ended the conversation. It had been a fruitful one, that was for damn sure.
My entire cohort was either gone from Nexus, or out of the industry altogether. That couldn't have been a coincidence. There was a driving force there somewhere, maybe sinister, maybe not, but definitely deliberate.
The pieces weren't connecting in my mind just yet, but I knew enough to get the feeling my hatred had been misplaced all these years.
Which brought my thoughts back to *her*.
Most of my lingering thoughts were of her lately. Her face. Her smile, rare as it was. Her voice; tight and cold with edges sharp enough to draw blood. Until she was happy, or amused, or aroused. Then it softened. I saw her lips. Her hair. Her legs and their adornments.
But at least the thoughts were fleeting.
The memories were worse. Insidious. They planted roots in my mind that grew into thick vines, wrapping all around me until I was completely immobile. I'd been trying to deny it to myself, but it seemed so plain to me now. There would be no freedom, not even after another night with her, because another night would only make me want her more.
Twice now, after being with her, I was completely satisfied for about five fucking minutes before the wanting started all over again.
I was the one who suggested this shit. I'd billed it as hate sex, because that's exactly what it was, but maybe it was more than that now. I wouldn't know for sure until I was standing in front of her, looking her in the eye. It was real easy to pretend otherwise in solitary moments like these.

I blew out a sigh as I watched my neighbor's dog pee on my mailbox. At least I had the next couple of days to myself. Maybe I'd get back on the apps and see what was out there. Maybe I'd even take it seriously going forward.

Yes.

I would take the first step toward the future, which definitely didn't include Electra Fucking Montrose.

28

Electra

I had my armor on tonight; a strapless full-length black dress with a cinched waist and a split. I hadn't had time to get my hair done, so I'd coaxed it into a deliberately messy updo with wisps hanging around my face. I wore the diamond studs my parents got me for graduation. I was ready.

My brother's wife was the first to approach me. No problem; she was a lightweight, emotionally speaking.

"Oh my gosh, Electra! You look gorgeous."

"Thank you, Cassidy. So do you."

We hugged gingerly to avoid smashing or smudging anything. Her dress was light pink and not really my style, but it suited her.

"I hate that we didn't get to talk at the anniversary."

I nodded, although my thoughts were the exact opposite.

"What's been going on with you?" she said as she locked arms with me. "The girls really miss you."

We walked toward the center of the room. The belly of the beast. "I miss them, too. Um, just work."

"Ah. Your little consulting thing, right? Are you still doing that?"

I gritted my teeth. "I am."

"Your mom said—"

"Oh, actually, let me go speak to her now. We'll talk later."

I broke away, but not to find anyone else in my family. The ballroom was full, but I managed to move through the room with detached ease, giving polite smiles and exchanging hellos with family friends and my father's coworkers.

I had almost reached the buffet tables when I heard the distress signal: "There's my Lex!"

I took a deep breath and turned. My parents approached me, hand-in-hand.

"Hey, Daddy. Happy birthday." I reached up and hugged him tight. "You don't look a day over fifty-nine."

His laugh bellowed in my ear. "Hush up, girl. Don't you look gorgeous?"

My mother looked me over. "Mm hm, you look pretty."

"Thank you."

Her eyes traveled north past my forehead and rested on my updo. "It must be humid today."

I gritted my teeth again. "Must be."

"No date?"

"Didn't know I needed one."

"You don't. Just asking." A tight smile followed. "Have you seen your brother yet?"

"No, but I saw Cassidy."

"Doesn't she look pretty? She went to Delores like I suggested." Her eyes went to my hair again. Delores was her hairdresser of thirty years. Looking at my mother's stiff barrel curls, I had no regrets.

"I'm gonna get a drink."

"Wait." She grabbed my arm and pulled me close. "Did you call Daddy's friend at the bank?"

"My job is going fine, Mama. Things are very much looking up."

"Up, as in...?"

"I'm doing well. I really am."

Her eyes searched me for untruths. "Well, good, then. I hope it works out."

I stared down at her hand gripping my arm. Symbolic of the hold she still had on me. My father, too.

"Okay. I'm gonna get that drink now."

She let me go with a nod, and I walked over to the bar with a new resolve: to get so drunk I wouldn't remember any of this. Things had started out tame, but it was only going to get worse from here, I knew that full well.

Halfway to the bar, I stopped cold and frowned, hardly able to believe my eyes.

It was *him*.

He smiled a genuine smile like he actually had some measure of affection for me. I was too stunned to return it, but he didn't seem fazed. His eyes followed me as I commenced my walk. By the time I reached him, I had my bearings again.

"Yes, it's really me. You're not dreaming."

I rolled my eyes. "What are you doing here?"

"I was in the neighborhood." He turned to the bartender. "Jameson, rocks, and the driest white you have."

"You were in the neighborhood," I repeated. "Looking like that?"

"Like what, Electra? What do I look like?"

I stared at him in black on black and sighed deep down in my soul.

Sex.

"Like you're on the way to somewhere."

He shrugged as he pulled out his wallet. He dropped a ten in the tip glass. "You seemed kinda down, and Nora told me it would be a nice thing to do. I figured since I'm such a good guard dog at work, I'd roll through and see if I was needed."

"You're never *needed*," I said with a smile. "I can't believe you really came here. On your own."

"That makes two of us."

The strangeness of the moment was interrupted by the bartender. Victor handed me my glass, picked up his own, and stepped closer to me.

"Cheers to the team."

"Cheers," I said.

Our eyes locked as we took the first sip. Our movements formed a mirror image. This was new territory for us, but we settled into the moment pretty quickly. By the time I finished half my wine, it felt like we'd come here together.

"So what happens at a Montrose party? Are all your family members as uptight as you?"

"Are all of your family members assholes like you?"

He pondered that. "Honestly? Yeah."

I stifled a laugh. "My father is cool. My mother is bougie and uptight—"

"Ah, okay. Tree. Apple. Got it."

"*Anyway*...my brother is hit or miss. And his wife is slightly annoying. I love them all, but...yeah."

His eyes roamed my face. "I get it. Family is complicated. You love 'em, you don't like 'em, they get under your skin. It is what it is."

"It's deeper than that."

"It always is." His eyes bore into mine. "You wanna talk about it?"

"Not really." I took several sips. "I still can't believe you showed up here like this. You're so...bold."

He nodded. "True indeed. That's one of the things you like about me."

"I don't like anything about you, Victor."

I flashed back to the other day in the car.

"Well, maybe I like one thing."

He chuckled. "I live to serve."

I looked away so he wouldn't see my smile.

"That feeling is mutual, though," he said, bringing my attention back to him. "It's real interesting to me. Your ice cold demeanor contrasted with that fire below."

My skin prickled. "I'm not cold. I just try to keep things professional."

"I told you on the plane. Cold and brittle. But that's not your only side. I see that now. I dig it."

I quirked an eyebrow. This was new. This was compliment circle reloaded. I wondered what it meant. If it meant anything at all. His showing up here had to mean something, but I didn't want to read into it right now. Too much to unpack.

"Electra. Who is this?"

Of course she found us. The woman had to have chipped me at some point. "Uh, this is Victor."

My mother's eyes scanned Victor from head to toe. She was good at analyzing people on appearance. I wondered what she saw.

"You didn't tell me you were bringing someone. Is this your date?"

"Um..."

"I am." He smiled warmly. "Nice to meet you, ma'am."

"Mrs. Montrose," she corrected. "Nice to meet you, as well. What do you do, Victor?"

"Victor works with me," I rushed out. "We're teammates on that project I was telling you about."

"I see." My mother's eyes raked over him again like he was the last St. John suit on the rack. "And how's that going?"

"It's going well. Your daughter has a mind for it. The clients are very happy with her work. So am I."

"Interesting." Her eyes narrowed. "Victor, is this your last stop, professionally, or do you have higher aspirations?"

I groaned internally. She was going in for the kill.

"Consulting? Absolutely. I have my own firm. Growth is always a goal, but I love what I do. I've always been a problem solver. To be able to do that *and* maintain my autonomy is the best of both worlds for me."

She turned to me. "See, when *he* explains it, it makes a lot more sense."

"I—"

"Sometimes when you have a passion for something, it's hard to explain," he said. "And it was very easy to explain to you, Mrs. Montrose. You aren't *my* mama."

Endra Montrose threw her head back and laughed. She laughed louder than I'd heard her do in a while.

That cinched it for me.

Victor Jackson could charm anyone.

My daddy walked over just then, undoubtedly having been lured by the siren sound of my mother's laughter.

"What's goin' on over here?" he bellowed.

"J, come meet Victor. He's Lex's date."

My father stuck out his hand. "Nice to meet you, young man."

They shook. "You too, sir. Happy birthday."

"Thank you." His eyes shifted over to me. "I didn't know you were bringing somebody."

"I—"

"I surprised her," Victor jumped in.

"Well, isn't that sweet," my mother cooed.

Victor put his arm around my waist. "Anything to see her pretty smile."

They ate that up, but I just stood there, frozen. His arm at my waist felt…normal, and his words made me smile. Mostly because I knew it was bullshit. Something about seeing my parents taken in by such an obvious lie was amusing to me.

"Alright, well, where's this brother at?" Victor said. "I'm locked in. Might as well meet the whole family at this point."

My mother laughed again. "He's over there."

Her hands gesticulated wildly as she hailed Emory, who came scurrying over with Cassidy on his heels.

For the next half hour, Victor spewed more bullshit and charmed them enough that they didn't notice me slip away to grab some food. I scarfed down the brisket, mashed potatoes, and vegetable medley—my father's favorites. I went back and made Victor a plate. I figured it was the least I could do after he showed up and rescued me.

Once the cabal broke up, I waved Victor over to my table and handed him his plate. I left him there for the cake cutting, then rejoined him once the DJ fired up the Frankie Beverly. Once the music started, my mother would order a daiquiri, and then she would get even more obnoxious, and I had better things to do. Even if I didn't, I wasn't sticking around for that.

I made my way back to Victor and picked up my clutch, which he'd been watching for me.

"You're ready to go?" he said in surprise.

"I am."

He stood with his empty plate in hand. "You headed home?"

"Why, did you have something else in mind?"

His lips curved into a smile as he stared down at me. "Lately, it feels like there's only been one thing on my mind."

"And what's that?"

He stepped forward, filling my space with the tall, handsome, sexiness of him. "Experiencing you again."

"Is that right?"

"Because that's what you are, Electra. A whole fucking experience."

I cleared my throat. "I guess I'm willing to give you another experience tonight."

"And I'ma give you one right back."

He grabbed my hand and led me out the door, dropping his plate into the trash can on the way.

We stepped out into the night, into air that was thick with heat and moisture and filled with the sounds of cicadas and frogs and birds who were obviously confused.

I empathized with those damn birds.

"I'm about five minutes up the street," he said, "unless you wanna go back to your place."

"Your place is fine. I'll follow you."

"Per usual." He smiled to himself.

"Keep on, Victor. I can easily go home."

"You can. But you won't."

"Oh, I won't?"

He squeezed my hand. "Nah. You want this as much as I do."

He gagged me a little with that one, if I'm being honest.

"I'm over here," I said as I dropped his hand. I hadn't even realized I was still holding it. It felt so natural.

"Alright, I'll walk you."

"It's fine, I'm right there."

"I understand that. I'm not sending you off by yourself, downtown at night. If that's okay with you."

"Fine."

He walked along behind me. "You love a fight, huh? That works out, cuz I love to tussle."

"I couldn't care less what you love. The only thing here is hate."

"Of course."

We both agreed, but neither of us sounded sure anymore.

29

Vic

She pulled in right behind me. I opened her door and helped her out, happy as hell that she was willing to give me the time. Popping up on her was risky as hell, but I had good intentions.

I was starting to realize I liked being there for her. I liked being around her. I liked looking at her, in various contexts. Seeing her in the office was something I looked forward to now. Seeing her on a Saturday night was a treat.

I opened my door and let her pass. "You want a tour?"

"No."

I laughed at that as I flipped on the lights. "Then I guess there's no need for pleasantries."

"None at all."

"Follow me."

I led her down the hallway and into my bedroom.

"Do I get the bed tonight?"

I shrugged. "If that's what you want."

"Oh, you care about what I want?"

I smiled. "We can keep doing this, but fair warning. My patience is thin right now."

"Date didn't go well?"

I loosened my tie. Slowly, like she liked it. Her eyes followed my every move, and I didn't miss the increasingly rapid rise and fall of her chest as she breathed.

"Honestly, I haven't really been in the mood for dates lately."

She took a pin out of her hair. It fell down around her pretty face and danced across her bare shoulders.

"I can see you having bad luck with women," she teased as she kicked off her shoes. "You're definitely an acquired taste."

"And here you are in my house taking off your clothes for me. Seems like you've acquired it."

She turned slowly, gesturing to her back. I happily took the opportunity to unzip her, peeling her out of her dress like a ripe piece of fruit. Silky brown skin greeted me, unencumbered by any lingerie.

My arousal heightened.

But when she let her dress fall to the floor, I saw that I'd misjudged.

There was lingerie, alright.

Black lace panties.

Black lace garters hooked to black stockings.

A low groan rumbled in my throat at the sight of her and *that*.

And the fact that she wore it, and walked around like that, having no knowledge that we'd be in this moment was so fucking sexy to me.

She turned to face me, her eyes falling to my erection. Mine went to her breasts. Round, smooth, and handful-sized, they stared right back, begging to be touched.

"Are you gonna take your clothes off?" She bit her lip, having no idea the state she was driving me to.

"I want *you* to do it," I admitted.

"No."

"No?"

"No."

"Come over here and undress me, Electra."

She put a hand on her chin, and the juxtaposition of her pose and her half-nakedness was funny. "Why would I just do what you say?"

I smirked. "I told you before. You want this as much as I do, sweetheart. Now, I'ma ask you one more time. Come undress me. Quit struggling and let me give you what you came for."

"Or, you could ask me nicely."

"Oh, *now* you want nice?"

Neither of us broke the ensuing stare, which seemed to last forever. Finally, I was the one to crack. It's hard to have pride when your dick is on brick.

"I can talk to you nice, Electra. But once I got you on that bed, I can't make no promises."

"I can agree to that."

"Would you *please* get your fine ass over here and undress me?

With a sigh, she closed the distance between us and went to work on my shirt.

I spent that time staring into her eyes and wondering why the sound of her nails clicking against the buttons of my shirt was turning me on so much. I stared down at her and resisted the urge to kiss all the lipstick off her lips.

I gave myself a quick mental reminder: *you hate this woman.*

My dick, though…he could go either way. He was angry, that's for sure, especially when she got my shirt off and brought her fingers to my belt.

That shit was torture. I was ready to bust, and she was taking her sweet ass time. Knowing her, it was calculated.

I watched her, relieved when she finally got my shit loose. I stepped out of my pants and boxers, gesturing to her to get on the bed. Ten seconds later, I was on my knees in front of her and placing her thighs on my shoulders. One finger slid her panties to the side. Two others made a home inside of her, finding her pussy wet and slick with need. My tongue went to work on her clit.

It was quick work. Enthusiastic work. Tasty work. She came with a desperate cry on her lips. When I stood and stared down at her, I felt grateful for my good fortune. Hate or not, it's not often you have a woman like her in your bed. As confident as I'd always been, I'd never aimed this high before.

I grabbed a pack of condoms out of my nightstand and tossed them on the bed. My next move was to climb on top of her, but once I did, I stared down at her face and realized I was on autopilot. This was usually the point where I kissed, but…we didn't do that.

She stared up at me with questions in her brown eyes. I didn't have any answers, so I hopped right back up and grabbed a condom.

While I rolled it on, she reached down and fiddled with her lingerie, unsnapping her panties on each side of the waist band.

I'd been wondering how to get her out of those.

That was easy.

A little *too* easy.

The garters, okay. But magical unsnappable drawls? You wear them shits for a reason. I started to wonder what her post-party plans originally were, but I immediately realized that was a road to nowhere.

I cleared my mind and settled on top of her, slowly easing myself in. We both sucked in a breath as I filled her up, then exhaled together when I came to rest.

I really shouldn't have, but I brought my eyes to hers. In the semi-darkness of my bedroom, the view wasn't perfectly clear, but it was intense. My dick got even harder, aching for me to move, but I just waited. Didn't even know what for. I just felt...content.

Her eyes shifted down to my lips, but she looked away immediately like she'd done something off limits. And maybe it was, to her, because I'd billed this thing as clinical and perfunctory, no romance allowed. Yet here we were, staring into each other's eyes. The line I'd drawn had already been crossed.

I let my eyes drop to her lips. Before I could stop myself, I raised my hand and placed my index finger in the middle of her bottom lip. A light touch, but I felt the impact. Her pussy clenched, giving my dick a brief hug that made me moan. I traced the heart outline of her mouth and made a decision.

I dipped my head and pressed my lips to hers. Her immediate response surprised me, but I had no complaints about her sliding her tongue into my mouth. None at all.

Our tongues danced as we swallowed each others' moans. It didn't feel like a first kiss at all. Like lifelong lovers, we'd done this a million times, it seemed. Her lips were greedy. Her tongue was playful. Her hands on my bare back were desperate and grasping.

I was overstimulated.

I had to move, so I did. I didn't break that kiss, though. My hands gripped her breasts; my fingers plucked and pulled at her nipples. Over and over, I stroked her and kissed her, a cycle of pleasure. Lather, rinse, repeat of moaning, stroking, licking, sucking, biting, gushing, fucking, *cumming*.

Yeah, there it was. It was so easy with her.

I only broke the kiss so I could talk to her. Softly, in her ear, I let her know, "I feel you, pretty girl. Cum for me. Just like that. You're doing so good."

Her moans were so loud, I wondered if she could even hear me.

"*Fuck*, it feels so good when you cum on my dick."

"Oh God. Yes…"

"Yeah, let it all out, pretty girl. You can say whatever you want when you cum." I pecked her lips. "I love them sounds you make. The faces you make. You're so fucking pretty when you cum."

My words of encouragement seemed to prolong her orgasm. Her pussy swelled and spasmed so hard, my nut rose before I even realized what was happening. I slammed into her and tried not to whimper as I came. The intensity of it shocked the hell out of me; I hadn't felt a nut tingle in my stomach since I was a teenager. With my face buried in her neck, I panted my way through it until the bittersweet end.

This was the part of the program where I was supposed to pull out and walk her to the door. But me being me—whoever that was at this point—I captured her mouth again and kissed her like she was the air I breathe.

I finally pulled away, rolling onto my back to stare up at the ceiling and contemplate my life.

"Do we still hate each other?" I finally said.

"As far as I know." She let out a sigh. "Although it's kinda hard to believe somebody who hates me could make me feel so good."

"What can I say? I was taught to be excellent in everything I do. That's an HBCU thing, you probably wouldn't understand."

She chuckled.

"But seriously, I don't know anymore. The way we fuck…the way you respond to me. It doesn't feel like you hate me. You don't taste like you hate me."

"Hey, look at me."

I turned my head to the left and met her eyes with mine. She smiled. "You're so handsome. Too handsome for your own good."

"Thank you. I think."

"You're a charmer."

"I'm just nice."

"It's more than that. I don't know why I was surprised my family liked you. They probably like you more than me at this point."

I frowned at that. "What's the deal with y'all?"

"Long, boring story. You don't wanna hear it."

"I asked."

She shook her head. "You're not getting everything you want tonight."

"I already did. I'm asking to listen."

"Not to entertain yourself?"

"I'm serious, Electra. You can vent if you need to."

"I appreciate that, but...I'm good."

She was comfortable behind her wall. If that's where she wanted to be, far be it for me to overstep.

Maybe just a peek, though.

"Well, whatever the deal is, your family seems solid. Good people. I can see why you are the way you are."

"How am I, Victor?"

"Head on straight. Ambitious. Poised. Respectable."

Her silence made me wonder, but all thoughts and questions left my head when she reached up and put her hand on my cheek. Maybe that's *why* she did it. Maybe I was getting too close.

"You kissed me," she said softly.

"I did. And you kissed me back."

"It felt good."

"I agree."

She rolled onto her side, lifting up to rest her body on her elbow. She stared down at me. "You know I'm a straight shooter."

I nodded.

"So, I want to say for the record that I like this."

"This being...?"

"The sex. It's amazing."

"Facts."

I waited for her to finish. After several moments, she smiled and said, "That was it."

"Okay, well, I like this, too."

Her fingers began to move, caressing my cheek absentmindedly while she said, "It's almost like…anything we do as a team goes really well."

"*Now.*"

"Right. Now."

"Honestly, you make it very easy."

I put my hand on top of hers, pressing her palm against my skin, stilling her fingers. It was intimate, but it felt right in the moment.

"Even though we hate each other, being around you sometimes is…very easy," I said. "Right now, for example."

"You mean *I'm* easy."

I laughed. "Let me engage my inner thesaurus real quick, because you, Miss Lady, are definitely *not* easy. No, what I mean is that I enjoy you. Even when we don't see eye to eye. Sometimes *because* we don't see eye to eye. You stimulate me. And not just physically."

"Same."

She leaned down and pressed her lips to mine.

That, too, was easy. Easy for me to slip my tongue past the seam of her lips. It tangled languidly with hers as I brought my hands to her back, wrapped them around her, and pulled her on top of me.

I immediately got hard again, and that fact wasn't lost on her. Heat enveloped my dick as she started a slow grind, rubbing her wetness back and forth, pulling groans out of me while her tongue swept my mouth hungrily. This cold, brittle woman was boiling over with passion. I'd never been happier to be wrong about someone.

"Don't play with me," I muttered against her lips. "Keep on and you gon' set off another round."

"Don't threaten me with a good time, Vic."

I nipped her bottom lip, then patted her ass. "Lemme grab another condom."

But she didn't move. Instead, she smiled sweetly and said, "Can you fuck me from behind?"

I wondered why she asked me that. Why *any* woman would ask that question expecting any answer other than, 'fuck yeah.' But me being me—whoever I was right now—I wrapped my arms around her and said, "At this point, I would do whatever you asked me to. And I mean anything."

"Seriously?"

"Yes, pretty girl. I'm the nastiest motherfucker you know, I promise you that."

It was a half-truth.

I'm nasty as fuck, but my willingness to fulfill her every desire had more to do with *her* than it did with me. She just...she inspired shit in me that I'd never felt with any other woman.

She rolled off me and got into position while she waited for me to strap up. I was opening the package when she looked back and said, "Me and Lance always used condoms."

I quirked an eyebrow. "And you're telling me this because...?"

"I've never had sex without one."

"Never?"

She shook her head.

"Are you sure?"

Her laughter made me smile. "I think I would know, Vic."

"So what are you saying?"

She *tsk'd* me. "I guess Howard doesn't teach deductive reasoning."

Sheeeee-it.

I tossed that thing to the side and lined myself up behind her, taking a generous moment to take in the sight of her. Naked skin. Soft, modest curves. That *lingerie*. And something new I discovered: a tiny heart tattoo on the back of her right shoulder.

I planted a kiss on it and then I did what I do.

That first stroke almost took me out. I paused, bit down on my bottom lip, and grabbed a handful of fluffy brown hair in my fist. This was DEFCON 5 level sex. The type of sex your uncles warn you about. That crashing out, turning on locations, driving by, popping up, making excuses, overworked, going broke, losing all your friends, crying in the dark, listening to Jodeci, begging on your knees type of sex.

I should have worn a condom.

This shit right here didn't make no kinda sense.

I stared at her ass, and the garters, and the stockings, and her waist, and my dick, and all the cream she leaked onto it, and shifted my gaze to the ceiling, hoping and wishing I could keep my fucking wits about me.

"What are you doing back there?"

Even her voice, that little edge in it, that annoyed twang, and her attitude...all of it. Allem. Every last one. Driving me out of my mind.

"I'm pacing myself," I gritted out.

She laughed at me. She knew I was back here struggling and she laughed anyway.

My girl.

I commenced to fucking her, pulling her hair like reins while she moaned and purred and screamed. I stared down at my little brown friend. That balloon knot was winking at me, so I licked my thumb and made a slow introduction.

"Oooohhhhh, Vic, what—oh my God!"

With my thumb secure, I palmed that ass like a bowling ball and went off, only slowing down when she busted, stroking her through it while I tried not to nut right behind her. I was enjoying this too much to stop now.

"Fuck, fuck, fuck...Vic...what are you doing to meeee?"

I wasn't doing anything to her that she wasn't doing to me. Still, my pride swelled at her words.

Once she was straight, I pressed her flat against the bed and rested my body against hers. I slowstroked her, losing myself in the warmth of her, drowning in extreme euphoria, an addict in the throes of his strongest high. But what goes up must eventually come down, and when I hit that peak, I pulled out of her despite longing to stay there forever. I was desperate for it, but I fell anyway, crashing back to earth with a roar. I spurted my cum on her ass, which she moved seductively while she moaned my name. Such a pretty sight. Like two glazed honeybuns.

I collapsed on my back next to her, throwing an arm over my eyes. At some point, I fell asleep, and when I woke up the next morning, she was gone.

I wanted to be mad, but I had no right to be.

30

Vic

The jacket, like everything else I owned, fit me like a glove. The trousers were a different story; the waist needed to be taken in a bit, apparently.

Taurus watched this from his pedestal, where another tailor buzzed around him. "You losing weight?"

"Nah. Been going hard in the gym. I might have lost a centimeter or two off my waist."

"Close to an inch," my tailor corrected.

"You training for something?"

I frowned at my big brother. "Quit interrogating me."

Isaac laughed from the cheap seats along the wall. His tux fit him just fine.

"What you laughin' at, man?"

"You seem agitated. What's wrong with you?"

I shook my head. "Just...got a lot on my mind."

"Work going okay?" Taurus said.

I waited while my tailor checked my collar. After he gave his final nod and walked away, I stepped off my pedestal and took a seat next to Isaac.

"Work is alright."

"Old girl still stressing you?"

I took a deep breath and exhaled slowly as I tried to figure out whether or not I wanted to talk to these unserious assholes about my feelings.

"Not really. We been…hanging out."

Taurus chuckled. "That's what we're calling it?"

"Whatever, man. I don't know…"

"Don't know what?"

"I think she got in."

Isaac slapped me on the back. "Victor's in love. Ain't that sweet?"

"Love? Who said anything about love? Nah, I'm saying I be thinking about her all the time. It was supposed to just be sex, and that's what it is, but I just…keep thinking about her."

"Sir, you can change out of it now. I have what I need."

Taurus nodded at his tailor and took a step down. He leaned against the wall next to me. "So y'all made up?"

"Not exactly. It's complicated."

"Uncomplicate that shit and ask her out. It ain't that hard."

"We've been out. Kind of. I popped up on her last week at a thing. It was whatever."

My brothers exchanged a look.

"I know what y'all are thinking. It ain't that deep."

"You popped up on her where?"

I didn't wanna say it, only because hearing it even in my head made me realize that it kinda *was* that deep.

"Her father's birthday party."

"You met her family?" Taurus' eyes were saucers.

"Yeah. And?"

Taurus crossed his arms in front of him, regarding me with a smirk. "That's interesting. I didn't even meet Savannah's mom until I was ready to propose."

"Nigga, that's you."

They laughed at that.

"I ain't never seen you like this, V. I'm concerned."

I looked over at Isaac and was met with the same smirk.

"Fuck you. And fuck you, too, Taurus."

"It's okay if you like her, man."

"Nah, you know what I like? The sex. It's flames. Okay? So y'all can kill the bullshit."

"If you say so, heart eyes ass nigga."

I stood and walked off to the changing room while they laughed at Isaac's dumb ass joke. That used to be me and him clowning Taurus on some getback for how he treated us while we were growing up. Now the tide had changed and I was the one caught under the wave.

Well, fuck them.

The only feelings I had for Electra were lust.

How could I have legitimate feelings for her after the way things had gone? It would be doomed before it started. All the hostility and hatred...there was no realistic way to get past that. Even her name was a fucking Greek tragedy.

Nah.

But I appreciated that little conversation, unserious as it was. It reminded me of who the fuck I am.

No more daydreaming. No more reading into shit that wasn't there. She'd made it clear last week when she snuck out of my place. It was just sex to her, so that's all it would be to me.

Back to business.

―――

"Okay, we're over the hump!" Nora announced.

We'd just submitted our gap analysis to New York, a major milestone. We had a presentation tomorrow, so most of our morning had been occupied by that. I always hated group work in school, and this was no exception, but at least I got paid for this shit now.

"I don't like these first four charts," Electra said as she frowned over my work.

"And those just happen to be the ones I worked on. What a shock."

Her eyes met mine. "Don't be so sensitive."

"Do you have an actual critique, or am I just supposed to read your mind?"

Nora sighed from over at her desk. "I think I'm gonna head to lunch early."

I laughed at that. "This is our process, Ms. Nora."

"Are we bothering you?" Electra said quietly.

Nora looked between the two of us with a sharp eye. "Yall bother me every day. I'm used to that. I'm just really hungry right now."

"Enjoy."

She threw up a hand at us as she exited.

I looked back at Ms. Trunchbull. "What's the problem with the slides?"

She shrugged. "I think green works better than blue."

"You mad about a color? What about the substance? The data?"

"That's all...adequate. The blue is the only thing throwing me off."

I shook my head. "You just wanna fight about something."

"No. If I wanted to fight about something, I'd tell you your cologne is way too loud today."

Embarrassed, I leaned away from her, almost involuntarily. When she saw it, she snickered.

"It smells good, it just smells like you took a bath in it."

Before I could clap back at that, a man came through the door. Tall, dark, and handsome, he towered over us. I stood to level the playing field, but he had me by a good three inches.

"You need something?"

He smiled warmly. "Here for lunch. How you doin', man? I don't think we've met. I'm Qadir."

"I'm Victor. What's that about lunch?"

Electra stood and grabbed her purse. "Let's put a pin in this, Vic. I'll be back in an hour."

Her devilish smile as she passed me was something out of a fucking horror movie. Jordan Peele himself couldn't have scripted this moment. A creepy slowed-down version of Forever My Lady played in my head.

Who the fuck was Qadir? Tall ass Qadir?

Just like that, they were gone. I returned to my seat, scratching my head about this shit. I should have taken my ass to lunch, but I wasn't even hungry anymore. I couldn't figure out why my heart dropped and my stomach sank.

But I tried to apply logic to it. They were just going to lunch. It's not like they could go off somewhere and—

Shit.

Yeah, they could.

I knew that firsthand.

But that didn't make sense.

I knew he had to work here. What department, though? I navigated to StarTech's homepage and tried to find the employee directory. You had to be logged in to see it.

I had credentials, but I also had PTSD. I wasn't e-going nowhere I ain't have no business e-being.

I closed out real quick and returned to my slides. After carefully considering Electra's point of view, I navigated to the design tab and changed the slide color from blue to a much brighter blue. After, I looked over at her laptop and realized she'd left it open and unsecured. In front of me.

That was new.

I worked through lunch. Still wasn't hungry until Nora came back with a styrofoam box that contained something that made my mouth water.

"What you got over there, Ms. Nora?"

She walked it right over to me. "Extra lemon pepper wings. You want one?"

When she opened the box, I felt like I was looking at porn.

"I'm too hungry for just one. Thanks, though."

"Take 'em. I was just gonna give 'em to Gerald anyway."

"Oh, nah. I can't take food out of your husband's mouth, Ms. Nora."

She laughed. "It's no problem. I'm cooking when I get home." She went back to her desk. "Does your girlfriend cook for you?"

I already had a wing in my mouth. I swallowed quickly. "Now you know good and well I'm single."

She cackled. "Well, it's your own fault."

"That's cold."

She went to speak again but stopped when a soft voice spoke just outside the door.

"Thank you for lunch. And dinner," it said, then came a flirty laugh. I leaned back a little, straining to hear, but a tall nigga's voice just sounded like low-pitched noise to me. Trying to be sexy noise. Macking noise.

My jaw clenched a few times.

Then Electra came prancing in with her own styrofoam box in hand.

I kept my eyes locked on my work, determined to keep my cool, but when she returned to her seat across from me, my cool found the nearest exit and took my dignity with it.

I crashed out.

"What's the deal with ol' boy?"

She glanced over at Nora, who had just put her earbuds in. "Who, Qadir?"

"The nigga that just took you to lunch."

"Lower your voice. I met him here at work."

"Y'all dating?"

Her eyes narrowed. "Why do you care?"

"I don't. I'm just curious."

"Why, though?"

"Can you answer my question?"

"Can you check your tone?"

I nodded. Fair enough.

"We had lunch," she said with a shrug of her shoulder. "He probably *wants* to date me, but he hasn't asked me out yet."

"What do you call going to lunch with him alone?"

Her eyes narrowed. "I call that my business."

I leaned closer and lowered my voice. "What if I told you it's my business, too?"

"That sounds like jealousy to me."

"Oh it absolutely fucking is jealousy. Do you think I wanna see you going out with other men?"

"Once again, that's *my* business, not yours. And I didn't think you would care, because all *we're* doing is having hate sex. Right?"

Something about the way her voice softened at the end made the question sound earnest, rather than rhetorical.

"Listen. You're right. It's your business. But I'ma tell you straight up." I lowered my voice again. "I don't wanna share you."

"Share me?"

"That's what I said. I'm selfish. Lawrence is one thing. I just pretend like he doesn't exist. But tall niggas coming by the office to snatch you up? That shit don't sit right with me."

"His name is *Lance*. And honestly, Victor, this is a bad look. I don't like possessive men."

I sat back in my seat and stared her down, pleased by my sudden realization. "Yes, you do."

She'd been working on her poker face. The only movement to be seen was a single blink.

"You could have met him at the lunch spot, but you didn't. You had him come by here because you wanted to see my reaction."

"You're talking crazy."

"Nah, I see you." A grin spread across my face. "Underneath all that prim and proper, you got a messy side."

"I do not."

"It's okay. I lowkey like that shit."

She squared her shoulders. "I'm not messy."

"Keep acting. Look, you wanted to see me riled up, right? You wanted my reaction? Here it is."

I leaned in closer. "I ain't sharing you, Electra. So I'ma let you decide. You wanna fuck around with other niggas, fine. But you won't see me again outside this office."

Anger flashed in her eyes. "Is that a threat?"

"It's a statement of fact."

"Do you think I need you?"

"Not at all. But I know you want me."

She pushed out a sarcastic chuckle. "You're so arrogant."

"Any man who can do what I do to you would be."

That stopped her, just for a moment. Then the mask went back on. "Whatever. You don't get to dictate who I see and don't see."

"Unless it's me. So you take all the time you need to think on that."

"I don't need to. I'll see who I want. As a matter of fact, maybe I'll ask Qadir out for this weekend."

"Cool. Have fun, and best of luck to that nigga in his future endeavor."

After a few seconds of silence, she laughed, which made me laugh, which made Nora take out her earbuds and say, "That Qadir is always sniffing around some woman in this building. I don't like him."

Electra put her face in her hands and whispered, "Shit. She heard us."

"Probably wasn't no fucking music playing in those earbuds."

She dropped her hands, bringing her eyes to mine. "Maybe it's best to just leave our...*situation*...in the past."

A million thoughts went on a rampage in my head, but I couldn't seem to organize them into a coherent sentence. Or one that wouldn't leave me looking and feeling like a damn fool. So I nodded and said, "Agreed," then I got back to work.

We didn't speak for the rest of the day.

31

ELECTRA

Things were back to normal with Victor. And by that, I mean we were back on each other's bad side.

And it was my fault.

The messy side of me—which he read expertly—was elated at his jealousy over Qadir. But the rational side of me was pissed that he gave me an ultimatum right after. I instinctively put my emotional armor on and raised my verbal weapons, because who the hell did he think he was making demands of me?

That night, my best friend answered that question for me in her own special Ciara way.

"Electra, sis, y'all are fucking. It's perfectly rational for him to wanna be the only one. Would you be happy if you knew he was fucking other women?"

I pondered that, then went on the defense yet again.

"But it was just sex. Hate sex. Which was his idea. I don't owe him a damn thing."

"Did he say you did? Listen, you wanted that man to react, and he did. You just don't like the reaction you got."

Once again, she'd rendered me silent, a silence that was only broken when she asked, "Do y'all ever get any work done, or do y'all just be fucking and arguing in front of that old lady?"

Crass as it may have been, it was the raw truth.

That *was* all we did, but it was working for us. So the question of why I pulled a stunt on him was still weighing on me a few days later. All throughout the week, we'd gotten plenty of work done. We were strictly business, and neither one of us had brought up the personal.

I'd been hoping he would, but no such luck.

I went to yoga this morning to clear my mind. It was adequate for the hour I was there, but as soon as I returned to the car, there was fine ass Freddie Krueger again, haunting my every thought.

Why couldn't I get him out of my head?

Despite my threat, I hadn't spoken to Qadir since our lunch. I'd even been dodging Lance's calls. Victor, who I hated, was the only man I had any interest in right now.

Surely that was indicative of something being deeply wrong with me.

After a dinner of chicken alfredo, I noticed I had a missed call from my brother. Reluctantly, I rang him back, thinking maybe he had something important to say.

"Hey, Em. What's up?"

"Hey, El. Nothing, just checking on you."

Turned out, he just wanted to see about me. That was a nice surprise.

"I'm good," I said with a yawn. "Was about to go to bed. What's going on with you? How are the girls?"

"They're good. In the bed. Probably not sleep."

I chuckled at that.

"As for me, I'm chillin'. It was good seeing you the other day."

"At the party?"

"Mm hm."

Okay, now it all made sense.

This was about Victor.

"It was good seeing you, too," I said. "Go ahead and ask me."

"Ask you what?"

"About my date. I knew you didn't just call out of the blue for no reason."

His raucous laugh rang in my ear. "I wish you didn't know me so well."

"Mm hm."

"He seemed like a good dude, based off those few minutes. Is this new?"

"I guess you could say that."

"The old folks were impressed."

"Now, that surprised me. I guess they only save their criticism for me."

"You know they just want the best for you."

"Best is relative, isn't it?"

He sighed. "They worry about us. Mostly you."

"You don't have to remind me of that, Emory."

"You put them through a lot. Let's not pretend otherwise."

"Why can't you ever be on my side? Aren't siblings supposed to do that?"

"El…"

"Is it hard for you or something? I don't get it. Never have."

Silence ensued. After a few moments, I made out the sounds of *Amen* in the background. My brother's favorite show since childhood.

"Ever since you went to seminary—"

"Don't start, El."

"It's true. And you know it."

"Well, you know what? Sometimes when we walk with people, the path diverges when we start to walk with God."

I sat up straight to hear him better. "Wow. So basically, I'm a heathen?"

"No, what I'm saying is that maybe our paths diverged a little. I'm okay with that. Are you?"

"I guess I have to be."

"You're my little sister. I love you with everything in me."

"Thanks, Em. It's great to hear those words."

"Do you love me back?"

"Of course. You're my brother. But someone wiser than me once said, 'Words are leaves fluttering in the wind, while actions are the roots that anchor the tree.'"

"You want me to do more, okay, I hear you. But what does that look like to you? I pray for you every night. I—"

"Prayers are still words, Emory."

He sighed. "I hear you. I do."

"Okay. Can you be my big brother for a second?"

"Yeah. I'm here."

I took a deep breath and blew it out slowly. "You really liked him?"

"I mean, yeah, from the little bit I saw."

"You used your discernment?"

He laughed. "I guess. You should probably be using your own, though."

"We're always arguing."

"Ohhhh, I bet you love that."

"What do you mean?"

"I hope it does work out, because you need an outlet for all that feistiness."

"Shut up."

"I'm so serious. I mean, I love it, cuz I'm your brother, but dating you…I'll just say I'm so glad you found your equal."

"Are you saying I'm—"

"I'm saying you're a headstrong woman, and I'm glad about it. But most men are too weak to deal with a strong woman. Victor seems like an equal. That's what I want for you. Him or whoever."

"I'm not *that* strong."

"You see? How you're fighting me right now?" He giggled like he used to when we were kids. "Don't ever change, El. I mean that."

After we said our goodbyes, I went right to my texts before I could talk myself out of it.

> I'm not going to date Qadir.

> Not because you told me I couldn't, but because I've assessed the situation and come to a logical conclusion

Conclusion about what?

> About which option I prefer

Prefer for…what?

> You really need me to spell it out?

Y-E-S

I rolled my eyes at that.

> I told you I liked what we were doing.

> Call me, I don't feel like texting all of this

Can't. I'm at the rehearsal dinner

> Oh. Well, enjoy

I'm sitting here texting you, so that should tell you how enjoyable it is

> Is it boring?

No, it's not that

You've been to one of these before, right?

> Yes

It's a joyous occasion, right? but all the love is amplifying my feelings of solitude

> I get that. I felt that way at my brother's event last month

Yeah. I'm physically present, but I'm emotionally disassociating

> Are you lonely?

...

I don't know how to answer that

> I'm being sincere, Victor

Okay then yeah. I guess. A little

My first instinct was to type, 'I'm sorry,' but that didn't seem appropriate, and I hadn't done anything wrong. But it pricked me a little to learn that he was lonely.

As I was conjuring up a response, he replied:

Anyway, what you up to tonight?

Men.

Can't stay in a feeling for more than sixty seconds. Or maybe he didn't trust me enough to be vulnerable.

Either way, the moment passed. At his request.

> Wedding's tomorrow, right?

It is

> Got a date?

Nope. Going stag

Why, you wanna pull up?

> I don't "pull up" but if you're asking me to accompany you, I would think it's a little late for that

The reception I guess, but not the wedding. It's at three at the botanical garden

No pressure

I laughed at the audacity.

The bride would have his head for inviting a guest at the last minute. Once again, MEN.

My laugh turned into a smile as I typed my last text of the evening.

> Enjoy the rest of your night victor

> You too E

I read it back several times. I suppose I was trying to recapture the feeling of warmth that swept across my skin the first time, but it wasn't the same.

Falling asleep was a chore. My mind was too busy. I turned from one side to the other searching for a sweet spot, but there was no relief. The internal debate was too loud.

The fact that I was considering it was remarkable enough to keep me awake. This was a man who had made me miserable twelve years ago, then spun the block and did it again. And yet...he'd also done things for me and *to* me that made me feel, well, decidedly not miserable.

I still wasn't sure I could trust him. Then again, I'd trusted him with my body. It wasn't too far of a leap to also trust him with my heart.

But something was blocking it.

The past, for sure.

We never got any answers, and until we did, this could never be more than what it was right now.

Oddly enough, I fell asleep just after I finally admitted that to myself.

32

VIC

THE GARDENS WERE BEAUTIFUL, the weather was mild and sunny, my brother was in love, and the bride was overjoyed. It was perfect in every way except for one thing.

She wasn't here.

It was stupid of me to expect her to be. Popping up at her father's birthday party was one thing, but a wedding was a whole other animal. And the night before?

Yeah, I was chasing waterfalls. Or windmills. Or both.

"You may now kiss your bride."

I looked away from the happy couple and locked eyes on my mama. The joy on her face made her look like she was shining. She never liked Taurus' first wife, but she loved her some Savannah, as well as her influence on my brother. It takes a special woman to tame the beast in a man, and he'd found her.

After the kiss, I slapped Taurus on the back.

"Congratulations, T. I'm proud of you."

He smiled and gave me a nod, then he led his new bride down the steps of the altar.

Naya followed, then Jordan, our cousin's son. I walked out next, linking arms with Bianca, the maid of honor. She was one of Savannah's line sisters, a tall, thick cutie with a doctorate. Good on paper and in real life, but I couldn't muster up a spark with her last night at the rehearsal.

We strolled down the petal-strewn aisle in awkward silence, heading toward the little office just off the path to wait for pictures to begin. It wasn't until we got to the end of the aisle that I saw *her*.

With her hair pulled back and black sunglasses covering her face, I almost didn't recognize her, not to mention the fact that she was ducked off in the very last row. It took everything in me not to drop Bianca's arm and make a mad dash toward Electra.

She smiled when she saw me.

A smile instead of a glare or a smirk.

It hit me then that we'd made extreme progress since we started this whole thing.

I dropped Bianca off at the office, relieved when the rest of the wedding party filed in behind us. At least she'd have somebody to talk to.

I made my way back outside and approached Electra slowly, wanting to savor this moment, although I wasn't sure why.

"You came."

She took of her sunglasses and stood. "Are you surprised?"

"Pleasantly," I admitted.

She smiled. "Well, you showed up for me, so I figured I'd return the favor."

"We're getting into dangerous territory here, showing up for each other."

"Don't get too excited. I'm mostly here because I love weddings," she teased.

"Well, either way, I'm happy to see you. You look beautiful."

She sighed. "You can't keep taking the sting out of my insults, Victor."

I laughed at that. "My bad." I stepped closer to her. "I'll make it up to you later."

"How will you do that?"

I looked around, appreciating the fact that we weren't in a church right now.

"I didn't forget that you expressed a strong desire to sit on my face."

She looked away as a nervous smile crossed her lips, brushing her hand over her hair, which wasn't even a millimeter out of place.

"When did you get here?" I said for a subject change.

"I was early. I saw you walk in. Looking all handsome in your tux."

"Thank you. You're coming to the reception."

"Are you asking me, or telling me?"

"Telling."

She shook her head at that, her face in an expression of tempered frustration like I was a child who misbehaved. "You can't spring an extra guest on them the day of."

"Let me worry about that, E. I wouldn't have asked you if I hadn't already taken care of it."

She looked skeptical.

"You trust me?"

"No."

I laughed. Of course she didn't.

"But it's a special occasion, so I'll make an exception just this once."

She didn't know it yet, but by the time the night was over, she was gonna trust me a whole lot more.

Taurus was pissed when I told him I might have a date coming. He didn't care personally, but he wasn't trying to stress his wife out the day before her big day. I understood that perfectly well and assured him that she probably wouldn't show up, but that if she did, she could have my food.

Then I fucked around and spilled about Naya. I didn't tell him everything, but when I saw her going down the aisle during rehearsal, I told him he should probably talk to her about how she was feeling about the baby. T seemed surprised by it, but he assured me he would talk to her.

Isaac told me I wasn't shit for bringing all that up the day before the wedding, and he was absolutely right about that. But perfect timing had never been my strong suit. My niece was hurting, and that was important. So, too, was Electra. Now *that* was an extenuating circumstance. They were men just like me; if they didn't get it today, they'd understand eventually.

"Okay, big smiles everyone."

Click!

My jaws ached from smiling. Thankfully, we were winding down. I was standing with my brothers watching the bridesmaids pose with Savannah when Isaac elbowed me.

"Who was that you were talking to?"

See, I wasn't even gonna bring it up. Today wasn't about me, and I'd already been annoying enough even mentioning it last night. So I shrugged and said, "Nobody."

My brother adjusted his glasses, giving me a stern look from behind the frames. "Was that her?"

Taurus tapped in, tearing his eyes away from his bride. "Her, who?"

"We don't have to talk about it right now."

"The hell we don't!" Taurus bellowed. He grimaced when he realized people were staring. "Nigga, you dropped that date shit on me at my rehearsal. See it through. Did she come?"

"Yeah, man. She's here." I shrugged. "You know how it is. Women love weddings. The romance and shit. I don't understand it, but, you know. So I was like yeah, you can pull up if you want to. And she did, so that's how she ended up here. Out there."

They burst out laughing.

"Ya mans is still in denial," Taurus said to Isaac.

"I hope the nigga got enough words left to give his toast."

"Denial about what?" I said, ignoring the jests.

"Clearly y'all are doing more than fucking if she showed up to this on short notice and you too scared to admit why you invited her ass."

"I don't know shit about that, but I do know one thing: I ain't introducing her to neither one of y'all niggas. Yall childish."

Once I got word we were done, I walked off to find the wedding planner to make sure she remembered to add an extra place setting for Electra.

Once we made it to the reception venue, just a few miles away, things progressed quickly. I didn't see Electra until after the wedding party was seated. After the toasts, I made sure Taurus was straight, then I dipped.

She was in the back along the side wall. Beggars can't be choosers, but I still felt bad about it.

When I told Yvonne to have my food sent to Electra, she laughed in my face and told me it wasn't that deep, and that there was plenty. That was a relief. I was willing to go back in the kitchen and pay the chef myself if I had to, but it worked out.

Her table was half-full, so I slid into the seat next to her and chilled there.

Once she finished, she pushed her plate away and patted her stomach. "I don't know if you know this, but I'm a foodie."

I smiled at her relaxed posture. "I know you damn near took my head off about them almonds."

"It was the principle, Victor."

"Uh huh." We shared a smile. "How did we get here?"

She frowned. "Where is here, exactly?"

"Comfortable. On a date. Enjoying said date."

"Well...sex, I think. That's where it started."

I nodded. "Where does it end?"

"Good question."

"Per usual."

She rolled her eyes at that, but it was playful this time. Her eye rolls were mostly playful at this point.

"I wanted to talk to you about something," I said. "I've been poking around trying to figure something out. Do you remember our cohort?"

She sat up and placed her elbows on the edge of the table, peering at me with curiosity. "Of course."

"I talked to O'neal a few weeks ago. That's when I found out none of us work for Nexus anymore."

"That doesn't surprise me."

"Would it surprise you to know there was some sabotage going on?"

"What do you mean, sabotage?"

"We know what happened with us. O'neal got investigated, too, after we left. Something to do with his non-compete. They got Xiang outta there on some xenophobic shit. Mario got straight up fired. And apparently Melanie quit over sexual harassment."

"I don't remember Nexus being toxic like that."

"How long were we really there, though?"

She inclined her head. "True."

"Listen. I don't know who did what. I'm only bringing this up with you because I think there's a very real chance both of us were innocent of what we were accused of."

She nodded.

"This is a cutthroat business. We were too green to realize we were walking into a den of vipers. Add to that the fact that we were part of a diversity initiative, and—"

"I see what you mean." She stared off into space for a moment. "What does it mean that we automatically blamed each other?"

"I haven't been able to figure that one out."

She clasped her hands together, but her fingers moved up and down. A nervous tic, it looked like.

"I wasn't really raised to trust people," she said. "I was raised to compete with people. Even my own brother."

I leaned in.

"Life as a black girl at an Ivy was very, very isolating. Instead of finding community with other people who looked like me, I tried my hardest to be better than them. To get better grades. Better connections. Better opportunities. Because that's what I was taught."

She sighed. "It doesn't excuse it, but I think that's my why."

I nodded. "I can see that. I appreciate you sharing that."

"What's yours?"

"Honestly? I just didn't like you."

She laughed.

"I'm serious. I liked everybody except you, so I figured it must have been you. My mind never even went to Nexus. That's on me."

"Well you not liking me is on me, so..." she trailed off, staring down at her fingers. "So then...we really have no reason to hate each other anymore."

"Even if we did, we wouldn't."

She held my gaze as she drank the last of her champagne, then turned to look at the revelers on the dance floor.

"I have a question," I said. "I want you to be completely honest with me."

She turned back to me expectantly.

"May I have this dance?"

Her smile warmed me. "You may."

I took her hand and led her to the dance floor. We wrapped our arms around each other and moved to the rhythm, losing time through songs I never heard. The only thing was her.

Until my mama interrupted.

"Victor? Who's this?"

We jumped apart like two teenagers who got caught kissing behind the bleachers.

"Hey, Mama. This is Electra. E, this is my mother, Ms. Jackson."

My mama gave her a once over, then pulled her in for a hug. It didn't take much with her, which is one of the things I always loved about her.

"Nice to meet you, Ms. Jackson." Electra's voice was muffled by the strong hug. After my mama let her go, she stood there all shy, and it was adorable. I'd never seen her like that.

"So...that's it? Can your mama get some details?"

"Sorry. We work together."

My mama reared back. "Work?"

"Well, obviously we're here together, but it's not...we're not..."

"It's new," Electra said with the save.

"Okay. Well, y'all are cute," Mama said. "Especially you. I love that dress."

"So do I," I said.

Electra thanked us both, then looked down at the floor. It was such a different side to her. I couldn't help but smile. She really was a marshmallow on the inside.

Mama went off to greet some people, then here came my brothers to ruin my fucking day.

I shook my head as they approached with identical giddy smiles on their faces.

"This 'bout to be some bullshit," I warned her, but she just stood there awestruck.

"What's wrong?"

She shook her head. "Did they make y'all in a factory? How are all of y'all this fine?"

Before I could answer, Isaac arrived first. "You must be Electra."

She looked at me. "You've been talking about me?"

"Well, yeah, I added an extra guest to the wedding, so..."

"Nah, nigga. Don't act," Isaac said, which made her laugh. "I'm his younger brother Isaac."

"Nice to meet you."

He sized her up as Taurus finally made it over. "Yeah, okay, I see the vision."

"Man, shut the fuck up. Taurus, this is Electra."

"Congratulations!" she said. "I'm so happy for you."

"Thank you, dear. I'm the oldest, by the way."

"Yeah, I can tell."

Me and Isaac busted out laughing. Electra immediately froze. I could tell she was mortified.

"Oh, God, I didn't mean it like...I'm sorry. What I meant was, you strike me as the most mature one."

"Aye!" I frowned at that. "I might be offended, too."

"Oh my—y'all, I seriously meant no offense. To any of you."

Taurus' frown broke into a smile. "We're just fuckin' with you. It's nice to meet you. Let me get my wife over here."

She turned to me. "You're mature, too, it's just—"

"You're good. It's all good. We clown in this family. You're fine."

After Electra and Savannah were introduced, I walked with Electra back to her table.

"I like your hair like this," I told her.

She swatted dismissively at her hair in the back. "It's just a bun."

"Okay, but I like that I can see your entire beautiful face."

"Oh, lord. The charm cannon is pointed at me now."

I laughed at that. "I mean, if you want hate, I can give you hate. I'm just being honest, though. I can't help it if you fine."

She grabbed my hand. "I want honest and authentic. So if that's hate sometimes, so be it."

I looked at her and smiled. "You know what? I agree."

33

Electra

I DIDN'T WANT TO see Lance anymore, I was sure of it. But that was a conversation for another time. Right now, there was only the afterglow. Side-by-side, Victor and I lay together, no words between us. What we'd just shared was quite a ways away from the hate sex we had before. This felt more like lovemaking, but can you make love *without* love?

A question for another time.

"I'm sorry for the way I treated you when we met."

Victor turned on his side to face me. "Where'd that come from?"

"I don't know. Just felt it, I guess."

"I get it. You were young. You had something to prove. We all did."

"Yeah, but I looked down my nose at you. I got that from my family, too. Not that that excuses it, but you can see the irony, right? They loved you."

He chuckled. "Why are they like that?"

"I don't know. They have extremely high expectations, and I haven't always met them." I took a deep breath. "I had a period where I disappointed them. A lot."

"What'd you do?"

"Okay, nosy." I shook my head. "They were so strict when I was growing up. I got to college and started wilding, basically."

His brow furrowed. "I can't see it."

"Good. It wasn't pretty. Drugs. Alcohol. A pregnancy."

His eyes widened. "You have a kid?"

My body tensed under the weight of that question. "No. I...lost it."

"Shit. I'm sorry."

I nodded. "It was early. Anyway, I lost my scholarship, and my dad had to call in favors and pay my tuition out of pocket. Hired tutors. Made me go to a women's retreat. It was a whole mess. And I guess the guilt of that, and everything they sacrificed to get me back on the right track...it's always stuck with me. So I guess I try my best to be perfect. Their vision of it, anyway."

"Damn. If I told my mama I was going to clown college, she would have bought me a red nose and sent me on my way."

I laughed at that. "Sounds like unconditional love and support to me."

"Yeah. Maybe." He stared into my eyes. "So who's the real you?"

"What do you mean?"

"I mean the you that exists outside of your parents' vision of you."

I rolled onto my side and propped my head on my hand. "I don't know how to answer that. Their vision was so bright, I couldn't see myself. Maybe I never really have."

"Can I tell you what *I* see?"

"Yeah."

"Obviously you're smart, beautiful, sexy as hell, feisty, fierce. Passionate. A little messy. Driven. But there's a softness to you. Which you told me about, remember?"

I nodded.

"You saw *that*, right? I'm sure there's more to you that you see. You probably just need space to think about it."

"Well, I love taking care of myself. My body. My mind. I do like being put together. That's my armor. And I think I can be sweet sometimes. But I'll never back down. It's just not in me."

"And I like that about you."

"Well even if you didn't—"

"Yeah, yeah. I got it. You don't care," he said, laughing. "And let me just say, I also apologize to you for my part in all this. The hostility and blaming you."

I stared into his eyes and found sincerity there. "It feels like a lifetime ago."

"Doesn't it?"

I wrapped my arm around his neck and pulled us closer. "But that's the past. We're right here."

"Yes, we are." His eyes dropped to my lips. "You know I can't get enough of you, right?"

"Is that right?"

He leaned in and nipped my bottom lip. "I'm hard right now. Again."

"Sounds like a *you* problem."

He groaned, then snatched me up and pulled me on top of him. "We're a team, so it's an *us* problem."

I sank down onto him, pulling moans out of both of us.

"Can you solve it for me, baby?"

I moved my hands to his chest. He did the same to mine. I nodded, and we made love again.

Love.

It didn't seem so farfetched anymore.

He beat me to work the next day, but I didn't mind. It gave me a chance to strut in and make my entrance, only now, I appreciated the way he stared, basking in the glow of his admiration and the way he optically consumed me.

No words were exchanged, but our shared looks communicated everything that needed to be said.

Someone knocked on the open door.

"Does Electra Montrose work in here?"

I turned around and waved at the man. "That's me. Do you need something?"

"Delivery."

He wheeled in a cart, upon which sat four gargantuan vases full of baby pink tea roses. Nora squealed and clapped her hands together, but I just stared as the man placed them on my desk.

Joy surged through me as I took in their delicate beauty. Their bright smell overwhelmed me.

"Enjoy, ma'am."

The delivery man left, and I began to search for a card. "Wait!" I called to him. "Did you forget the card?"

He turned and shrugged. "No card. Must be a secret admirer."

Nora's eyebrows raised. "Qadir?"

I doubted that. The only men on this earth who knew my favorite flowers were my daddy, Lance, and Victor. My dad would have included a card for sure. Lance didn't have my work address. That only left one, and judging by his complete non-reaction, his lips appeared to be sealed.

"Maybe," I said to her, my attention returning to my lovely flowers. "Whoever it was, I guess he wanted it to remain a mystery. But I hope he knows how much I love them."

He didn't turn around, but a few moments later, I got a text.

Their beauty pales in comparison to yours

Oh, he was applying pressure.

34

Vic

A WEEK AFTER OUR presentation to the executive board, I was called into a closed-door meeting with Carter Wells. Electra wasn't copied on the invite, so I kept it to myself, not wanting to alarm her. I had no idea what it was about, good or bad, so my nerves were shot.

I arrived five minutes early for our ten a.m. meeting. Carter was already seated, so we got started immediately.

"Victor, I want to say off the bat that this is a friendly meeting. Just talking."

I relaxed a little. "Okay. About what?"

"Your FOCUS model. We were very impressed."

"Oh. Thank you."

That surprised me. Electra and I came up with it the night before the presentation, almost as a throwaway. FOCUS stood for Framework for Operational Consistency and Unified Strategy, and it was a bespoke process model for StarTech's first stage of strategy. There were two slides on it. We hadn't even fleshed it out.

"We're so impressed, we'd like to make you an offer."

I had to think about that for a moment. "FOCUS isn't for sale," I finally said.

He smiled. "Of course. We want to bring you in-house for implementation. This project is ongoing, obviously, and it makes more sense to hire you than to have to renew and renegotiate your contract every time." He smiled. "We would make it worth your while, I promise."

"I believe you. What about Electra?"

"What do you mean?"

"FOCUS is a collaborative effort between the two of us."

"Ah. Well, once her contract is up, we will not be looking to hire her in-house. As far as the IP, that would up to you two to sort through."

I swallowed hard. What I'd just heard had my head spinning.

"Sorry, I need to think about this."

"Of course. Take a few days."

"When you say worth my while…"

He opened a manila folder and pulled out a single white sheet of paper. He slid it across the mahogany table, and I stopped it with my finger. The number made my blood run cold.

"You'll have my answer tomorrow."

Back in our office, I folded the sheet and stuffed it in jacket pocket. Nora looked up at me as I passed by her, her face going slack when she saw me.

"You okay?"

I stopped and glanced over at Electra. She was deep in her work. I shook my head as I approached Nora. "Did you know?"

"Know what?"

I looked behind me, relieved that Electra wasn't paying us any mind.

"They offered me a position," I whispered.

I could tell by her slumped shoulders that she was involved in this. Her eyes cut to Electra, then moved back to me.

"There was a memo."

"When?"

"After the presentation," she said. "I got copied on it. It was mostly just notes, but then people started replying all. Of course."

"So you were copied, and you had no input."

Her eyes widened. "None at all. I give you my word."

"You weren't gonna say anything?"

She sighed. "Victor, as much as I enjoy working with you, I'm employed by StarTech, not you."

"Fair enough." I couldn't be mad at her for that. This was business, and I wasn't the one cutting her checks.

She looked over at Electra again. "Did you accept?"

"Not yet."

"It's tempting, I know."

"I don't think you have any idea how tempting it is. My name is mud in this industry, Ms. Nora. This is what I've been working for."

"Well, I wish you luck with whatever you decide. I'm sure you'll make the best decision for you."

That sounded pointed to me, but I may have been projecting. Either way, I needed to talk to E about it.

I walked over to her and touched her back gently.

She looked up and smiled, looking absolutely beautiful surrounded by those pink flowers. It could have been a painting. My own personal Mona Lisa, but black and way badder.

"What are you working on?"

She sighed. "Finishing up the market research. I'm tired already."

"Are you at a place where you can stop?"

She frowned. "Yes...what's wrong?"

"I need to talk to you about something."

"Okay..."

Behind me, Nora cleared her throat. "I'm gonna run down to the cafe. Anybody want anything?"

We both shook our heads.

Once she left, I rolled my chair over and sat across from Electra, just like we had the day we did the trust exercises.

I was probably about to undo all that.

I took a deep breath and let it out slowly. The nerves were unexpected and irritating, because they spoke to exactly how invested I was in the outcome of this conversation. And that was very uncomfortable to acknowledge.

"I met with Carter Wells this morning."

Her face fell. "Why? What did he say?"

"The work is good. He's happy about it. They all are."

She exhaled. "Okay, then why do you look so down? And why did he only meet with you? When was this even scheduled? You didn't mention this to me."

Might as well rip the bandaid off.

"Okay, look. They loved FOCUS."

Her brows furrowed over her pleased smile. "FOCUS is kind of trash, though."

"Well, they loved it so much, they wanna hire me on for implementation."

Her eyebrows raised slightly, a question I couldn't answer without breaking her heart.

"Just me."

The change was immediate. I didn't just see it, I *felt* it. The wall we'd slowly dismantled over the last few weeks was hastily erected all over again.

"Electra, I know—"

"If you think I'm giving up my half, you're out of your fucking mind."

"That's not what I was gonna say at all. If you'd just give me a second, I—"

"Did you tell them we came up with it together?" she said, her voice going shrill. "Did you bother to confess to that, or did you just sit there and let him gas you up?"

"I told them!" I answered, my own voice raising. "You honestly think I'd try to steal an idea from you?"

"I don't know what you'd do," she spat. "So what'd you tell them, Victor? When do you start?"

"I—"

"How did you expect me to react to this? Hm? Did you think I'd be happy for you? Just because we've been messing around? Well, I'm not. I'm *pissed*. And I'm not gonna be gaslighted out of having an honest reaction to this bullshit."

"Ain't nobody—look, stop interrupting me and let me say what I have to say."

"Unless you're gonna tell me you're turning it down, I don't wanna hear shit."

She stood and grabbed her purse. "Matter of fact..." she trailed off and stormed off. Her heels sounded like gunshots on the hardwood floor. I stared after her, dazed and confused.

"Electra, wait!" Nora's voice sounded just outside the door. She entered and looked right at me. "What'd you say to her?"

"I didn't get a chance to say much of anything before she flew off the handle."

She waved a disapproving hand at me. "I should have given you a script."

"For what?"

Exasperated, she shook her head. "What are you doing tonight?"

"Shit, I don't know. Begging?"

She burst out laughing. "No. You're coming to my place for dinner. Seven o'clock."

35

ELECTRA

I RANG NORA'S DOORBELL at seven-fifteen. It took her a while to answer. I stood there for at least a minute sweating and dodging moths.

By the time she finally answered, I was even more agitated than I was when I left work.

"I'm so glad you made it. Come in, sweetheart."

The smell of something cooking hit me immediately. A homey smell. I breathed long and deep. It reminded me of my parents' house.

The house looked homey, too. I wondered if she specifically searched for that in an air b&b.

Victor stood when he saw me, as did an older gentleman who I knew must be Gerald.

"Honey, this is Electra, the one I was telling you about. Electra, this is my husband, Gerald."

Ignoring Victor, I stuck out my hand and exchanged a shake with Gerald. After, Nora herded us all into the dining room where we sat at the empty table.

"Okay, first things first," she said. "We're gonna eat, but we're gathered here today because I wanted to get y'all off of StarTech property so we can have a real conversation."

"About what?"

She glanced at Victor, then back at me. "Okay, here's the deal. I've been at StarTech a long time. I'm a good employee. I do my work."

Gerald nodded along.

"But I don't have an allegiance to them. I haven't known you two long, but I feel more of an allegiance with you. So I'm gonna give my opinion, if that's okay."

We both nodded our agreement.

"It's a corporation. It doesn't care about you. It cares about profit. And that's what this is all about." She looked at Victor. "I don't know what they offered, but I can guarantee you, it's a fraction of what they stand to gain. My guess is that once they hand you that contract, it'll contain all kinds of subtle, sneaky language about taking ownership of your intellectual property."

Victor smiled.

"I know you can't patent or trademark it, but you need to write up every last detail tonight and copyright that writing. Then, you hit StarTech with an NDA. Then—"

"I'm one step ahead of you, Ms. Nora."

She smiled. "I'm not surprised."

He turned to me. "Can we talk? And by that, I mean can we talk in a way that actually lets me get my points across?"

"Fine."

He glanced at Nora, probably expecting her to give us some privacy. She just stared back. It was her house, after all.

"Look," he said. "After everything that's happened, I thought we got to a place where we trusted each other. But clearly, you still have reservations about me."

"Actually, I don't. I was just pissed. And hurt."

"I understand that."

I exhaled, expelling my hurt and anger. "I'm sorry I lashed out at you. And I do…" I trailed off. "I'm trying to trust you completely. Personally, I do. Professionally, I'm trying to get there."

The hurt in his eyes bothered me.

"What do I have to do?" he asked. "I thought we were…" he shook his head. "You know I have feelings for you, right? Surely you know that."

I glanced at Nora, who was smiling like it was Christmas morning. "I have them for you, too. It's just that…it's hard to separate personal from business. And I need to know how you handled this. I just do."

"I understand, but you're acting like I didn't try to tell you four hours ago. I'm trying to tell you right now."

"You're right. I'm listening."

He took a deep breath. "I considered it."

My blood ran cold.

"Accepting that deal would go a long way to securing my future," he continued. "Hell, it *would* secure my future. Seven figures worth of it."

Damn.

No wonder he didn't immediately decline and storm out of there. I wouldn't have, either.

He grabbed my hand and laced his fingers through mine. "The problem, as I see it, is that lately, whenever I think about my future, all I see is your face."

Nora made a quiet squealing noise. Gerald shushed her, which made Victor chuckle.

He turned back to me. "Baby, it's not a clear picture. Yet. I don't know exactly where I'm going, but I know whenever I start making moves, I want you by my side."

"So you're turning it down?"

"Not exactly." He reached into his inner suit pocket and pulled out a tri-folded packet of papers. "I saw an attorney friend of mine. I had him draw up a partnership agreement. Equal shares. Equal ownership of FOCUS. Equal ownership of our firm, whatever we decide to name it."

"You wanna be partners? Since when?"

He unfolded the paper and laid it flat in front of me. "Since we became a team and started killing this shit. Did you not hear me say seven figures?"

I stared at the paper in disbelief. The words blurred together on the page. "My head is spinning."

"But listen. If you don't wanna be my partner, I can also buy you out."

He pulled out another stack of papers. "We'd have to negotiate a price, of course, but this way, you don't have to be tethered to me past the end of this project. If you don't wanna be."

I felt like a zoo animal. Three sets of eyes all trained on me like rifle scopes. I closed my eyes, comforted by the gentle squeeze of Victor's hand.

I opened my eyes and looked around.

"I can't decide this with y'all staring at me."

They all laughed.

"I don't like being in this position," I admitted. "This is the weaker position. I've been running my own business for ten years. I only answer to myself."

"Equal partners, E."

"But what if things don't work out on the personal side?"

"That's fair. But what if they do? What if I make you happy? What if we fall in love? What if I give you the world? There are several possible outcomes here, E."

"I know. I just...I don't know."

"What are you scared of?" His voice was soft and gentle. "Be honest."

"I don't know."

His eyes searched mine. "Baby, stop fighting." He dipped his head, forcing himself to my level. "You don't have to fight anymore."

It was the way we started. It was what I knew.

I was a fighter. I would never change. But maybe I didn't have to fight this. Maybe Victor and I would fight together. Although it's a corny platitude, maybe 'us against the world' could be the story we'd write.

I leaned in and pecked his lips.

"We better get to work."

"What are you doing? We're supposed to be working."

I tightened the death grip I had around his neck and planted soft kisses on it. I'd been so good for the first hour or so we'd been working at his place, but out of nowhere, the urge to make love hit me and I hopped out of my seat and onto his.

"Electra..." he sighed as his hands moved to my back. "This is very distracting."

"It's supposed to be."

He chuckled. "Now, see, you bout to get yourself in trouble."

"Good trouble."

"Mm hm. Look at me."

I did, and what followed was a soul-shattering kiss that took my breath away and confirmed to me that this was exactly where I was supposed to be.

But then he pulled away.

"As your partner, I have to say, I think your work ethic leaves a lot to be desired."

I made a face at him. "I know what you desire. You think I don't feel that?"

"Baby, my dick is always hard around you now. We still got work to do."

"How about a quickie?"

"You need some discipline."

I bit my lip. "Ooh, I agree."

"No, not—" he burst out laughing. "I hate you. Go sit over there before we fuck up this deal."

I pouted, but he was right. For once. So I put some distance between us in service of the business.

There were seven figures on the table.

We could make all the love we wanted once the deal was done.

36

ELECTRA

CARTER WAS SURPRISED TO see Victor and me walk into the conference room together. Back where it all began.

He stood to greet us, his confusion palpable. "Oh, hi. What's—I didn't realize we were meeting about the current project."

"We aren't," Victor said. He pulled out my chair and got me settled before taking his seat. Then we waited.

Carter looked back and forth between us. "Oh. Okay. Um..."

Silence.

Victor made him wait an uncomfortably long time before saying, "I asked to meet so I could give you an answer."

Carter's eyes shifted to me, then back to Vic. "I think I have an idea."

"Ms. Montrose and I are now fifty-fifty partners in a new consulting firm. Montrose & Associates. FOCUS is copyrighted IP designed under that brand."

Carter chuckled dismissively. "You can't copyright a model, Victor. Surely your attorney advised you of that."

"He did."

Carter spread his hands. "Then what are we talking about?"

Vic pulled the papers out of his briefcase and slid them across the table at Carter. Seemed a little rude to me, but men do things differently. And get away with it, too.

"Obviously, the process is on record as having been written first by Ms. Montrose and me. Your employees are welcome to use company time to memorize all forty-six pages, but that seems cumbersome to me. Now, with that said, M&A accepts your offer to oversee implementation."

Carter's eyes dropped to the papers, then rose immediately again like the very act of seeing them was offensive.

"I made the offer to you."

"I'm no longer just me. If you want to keep FOCUS in-house, this is the way it has to be."

Carter leaned back in his chair, all pretense gone now. "May I speak frankly?"

"Please."

"If we wanted to make an offer to Ms. Montrose, we would have."

Victor's eyes narrowed. "Ms. Montrose is an equal partner. She's also sitting in the room with us. Please show her the proper respect by addressing her."

"Very well." He looked at me. "If I wanted to make you an offer, I would have."

Victor chuckled. "Yeah, I don't like that."

"I did exactly what you asked."

"And it still felt disrespectful."

"Were you unsatisfied with my work?" I cut in.

"Not at all. To be frank, again, it's not personal. We simply don't need two of you."

It took everything in me not to ask why it was Victor and not me. It would have been pointless, though, because truthfully, I knew the answer. Victor did, too, I'm sure. He'd read the articles.

"Well, we aren't asking you to double the offer," I said. "That would be ridiculous."

"Yes, it would." Carter stared at me, his eyes narrowing into slits. I knew that stare. I'd seen it a million times. It intimidated me until I realize that was exactly what it was designed to do. After my realization, I simply mirrored it back to them.

Like now.

"Just out of curiosity, why Montrose & Associates?" He looked over at Victor for the answer.

I turned to look at him, as well.

"Because that's what Ms. Montrose wanted. She gets what she wants."

I turned back to Carter and smiled.

He inclined his head up and raised his eyebrows at the same time, universally known as a *that's bullshit* gesture. But that was fine. He didn't have to understand it. His only task today was to sign these fucking papers.

"Obviously, I'll have to run this by the team leads."

"Obviously," I agreed.

"And if we agree, our lawyers will have to draw up new papers."

"Of course. Those are provisionals. There's an LOI in there as well," Victor added. "We'd like to get that signed today."

Carter sighed with all the impotent anger he could muster, but he sure pulled that pen out of his pocket.

We waited a while for him to read through the thin packet. It wouldn't be a done deal until his attorneys and HR got involved, but the LOI would give us room to breathe.

Victor caught my eye, giving me a covert smile that made my insides tingle. The picture was beginning to clear for me. No more confusion, no more obfuscation. No more denying it to myself. He was my future.

Finally, Carter signed, darn near digging ditches in the paper with all the pressure he put on the point.

I used to worry about that, too. How do they feel? Are they mad? What's gonna happen? But I realized I was expending way more emotional energy on these situations than they ever were. And at what cost? Stress. Lack of peace.

It was for the birds. Truly. I never felt more free than I did the moment I stopped caring about feelings. There's no crying in baseball, type things. Men in business don't care, so why the hell should I?

In fact, I hoped Carter *was* mad. Let him feel something. Let him carry the weight of being outgunned. Let him worry about what he could have done differently. It wasn't my burden to carry. Never was.

"Okay, then!" he shouted. "You'll be hearing from us!"

I bit back a laugh.

We stood and shook hands, waiting for him to leave before we turned to each other and hugged it out.

"Congratulations, baby."

I gave him a quick kiss. "Congratulations, babe. We did it."

"We did." He gave me a final squeeze, then let me go. "You ready to go celebrate?"

"If you're asking if I'm ready to suck your dick and swallow every drop, then yes, I'm ready."

He stopped walking and turned around to glare at me.

"What?"

He shook his head as the smile spread across his face. "I just...really didn't think you had all this in you."

"Nah, I'm hateful, remember? Wait and see. I'm sucking that thing like I'm mad at it."

He burst out laughing as he ushered me out the door. "Don't ever change, E."

A week after our final paperwork came through, Victor and I had dinner at my parents' house.

It was a milestone for us. We'd made it official, and although we didn't talk about it much, we both knew where things were headed.

For now, though, we were enjoying the ride.

Victor turned on his one-man show during dinner, charming them and keeping them all in stitches and away from the subject of me. But it was okay, today. I finally had some good news to share.

"So, I have an announcement," I said as Cassidy cleared the plates. "And something I want to give you," I said to my parents.

"Basically, Victor and I have gone into business together. We started our own consulting firm."

My mother raised her eyebrows. "Really?"

"Yes. Really."

"Is this because you think you'll be more successful with a partner?"

"I *am* more successful with him. So much so, I have this for you."

I pulled the check out of my purse and passed the envelope to Vic, who passed it to Em, and around and around it went until it got to my mother.

She gasped when she opened it. She stared for a few moments before shoving it into my father's hands.

"I appreciate everything you all did to get me here, but it was time."

"Sweetheart, you didn't have to—we're your parents," my father explained. "It wasn't a loan."

"No. It was an albatross."

"Excuse me?" Both of their mouths dropped open.

"Maybe you didn't mean for it to be, but it's always felt like that to me."

Mama shook her head. " I don't think so. You felt burdensome, and then you projected it onto us."

"If that's the way you want to spin it. Sure."

"Wait, go back," my father said. "This new company. How is it all of a sudden so successful? And right out of the gate?"

Vic entered the ring. "Because your daughter is so smart and resourceful, she came up with a process model our client was willing to pay a lot of money for."

"We came up with it together," I corrected.

"But it was mostly her."

"It was *not*. It was equal."

He looked over at me. "Can it ever really be completely equal, though? Unless you're sitting there measuring it out, you can't say for sure."

"Okay, but you can say for sure that I had more input? I'm not saying I didn't—"

"That's exactly what you said."

"Whatever," I huffed. "The point is that—"

"I think the point here is that both of you have met your match."

We both looked at my brother.

"What?" he said with a cheeky smile. "This is good, I like it. Keep going."

"Electra, sweetheart, we don't need your money."

My attention turned back to my mother. "I know you don't. But it's something I need to do for me. You can put it away if you want. Give it to my kid one day. If I have one."

"Kid? Okay. That's new." She looked at Victor. "What are you doing that has my daughter thinking about kids all of a sudden?"

Victor looked at me. I looked at him.

My mother, realizing her mistake, said, "Oh, no," while my father and brother both groaned loudly. Cassidy, who had stopped moving to listen, cackled loudly behind us.

"I think this conversation is over," my daddy said in disgust. "We'll put this money away. The end."

"Sir, I—"

"Victor, I like you, son. You're a fine young man. Don't say nothin' else, hear?"

"Yes, sir."

And that was the end of that.

Later, at his place, Victor spilled his kids all over my back and down my throat.

It was a fitting end to a night on which I felt reborn. Free. Free to be exactly who I was.

And I had a man who loved all of it.

37

EPILOGUE

Six Months Later...

"Ms. Montrose, I have a bunch of documents I need you to look over and sign."

I looked at him across the conference table of our new office building. We still had boxes to put away, but it was all ours.

"Mr. Jackson, can it wait? I'm booking the flight right now."

"Oh! I meant to tell you." He closed his laptop and came to sit beside me. "I know you'll probably think this is dumb, and it'll cost us more money, but how would you feel about us booking separate flights?"

I stopped what I was doing and looked up at him. "Separate flights?"

"I know. It's morbid, but if something happened..." he trailed off and rapped his knuckles on the oak table. "Our shit's too profitable, you know what I mean? Key man risk and all that. What do you think?"

I burst into tears.

Victor's eyes got big, and his arms immediately wrapped around me. "Baby, I'm sorry. I know you don't wanna think about it, but it's real."

"No, it's not that," I sobbed into his chest. "This is what I wanted."

"For us to die?"

"No!" I pulled back and swatted his shoulder, laughing and crying at the same time. "I always envisioned having a company with partners that's so big we have to fly separately, and now we have that."

"Oh. Damn. Well, good?" His face was creased with uncertainty. "You sure you're okay?"

"I'm happy, I swear." I wiped my cheeks with the back of my hand. "It's just...it feels weird to actually get something you wanted so bad."

His expression softened. "Yeah, I feel that."

He reached over and grabbed a packet of papers. "Speaking of things we want..."

I looked down at it. It looked official. "What is this?"

"Read it."

I sniffed and looked around the room for tissue. We had a box here somewhere. "I'm busy, Vic, can you just give me the cliffs?"

"Is that what they teach you at the Ivies? How to take shortcuts?"

I rolled my eyes. "I don't have time for your foolishness today, Mr. Jackson."

"I'm really gonna need you to look over this one."

"Ugh. Fine."

He stood and walked away while I read the name of our attorney on the front page.

My heart sank, thinking we were being sued for something, but as I flipped to the second page, I realize this was something very different.

My head popped up. "Victor!" I shouted. He was nowhere to be found.

His footsteps approached quickly, then he rounded the corner.

"I was coming right back, babe. Here."

He set a box of tissue in front of me, but that was the last thing on my mind right now.

"This is a prenup," I said as I tapped the papers. "A prenuptial agreement."

"I know." He pressed a button on his phone, and SiR began to play. He reached into his suit pocket and pulled out a velvet box.

"Oh my God. What are you doing?"

He smiled as he went down on one knee. "Electra Fucking Montrose."

I laughed as tears welled up in my eyes.

"You are truly something else. I was planning this big romantic, public proposal. I thought that shit up months ago, but I realized pretty quick that none of that is you."

I nodded.

He stared up at me, gazing lovingly through black lashes. "I learned what romance is to you. It's being successful."

I laughed again, wiping tears away.

"It's security. It's having everything in a row, lined up neat where you can see it and you know what's gonna happen. Baby, you like perfection because you *are* perfection. Not literally," he emphasized with a grin, "but for me."

He opened the box, revealing the biggest, shiniest rock I'd ever seen in real life. *It* was perfection.

"Baby, you are the love of my life. My partner. In everything. I don't know how hate turned into love, but I thank God it did. I don't know what I would do without you next to me."

He took a deep breath and blew it out. "Okay. I'm almost done. Lemme get through it. Electra, everything you need is in those papers. What you come in with, you keep. I want forever, but I know you, and I understand you, and you get whatever you want, pretty girl. So it's laid out in there for you, so you feel safe here. I want you to feel safe and secure with me. So with all that said, will you please be my wife?"

"Yes, yes, yes, of course."

I threw my arms around him and cried. He went through half the box trying to wipe my tears, but I couldn't stop crying. He slid the ring on my finger, then he cried a little. It wasn't Paris or Italy or over the intercom at a stadium during a game in front of thousands, but it was perfect. It was the most romantic proposal for me. This man understood me. He *got* me. He loved me, flaws and all, and he gave me exactly what I needed.

After we called our parents, he laid me out on the conference table and sealed the engagement with four orgasms.

It was rough, too. Aggressive.

I love the way he hates me sometimes.

THANK YOU

Thank you for reading! If you enjoyed this novel, please consider leaving a review on Amazon or Goodreads so other readers can enjoy it, too!

Join my mailing list to be notified as soon as the next book is released, and to learn about other upcoming novels, giveaways, freebies, and more.

CLICK TO JOIN

You can also find me on Instagram. And my website. And Twitter. And TikTok.

About the Author

Shae Sanders grew up sneaking her sister's Jackie Collins novels when she really didn't have any business reading them. But they stoked a love of edgy and steamy romance against the backdrop of business and power. Now, she writes about black love, lust, and relationships with a side of social stuff thrown in for a little razzle dazzle. In her spare time, Shae spends time with her kids, watches her favorite shows over and over again, and teaches as an adjunct professor.

BOOKS BY SHAE SANDERS

Standalones

First Class Love

Love and War

Santa's Helper

Sand to the Beach

Act Like You Mean It

The Replacements: A Grumpy Boss Romance
Studio 79

The Happiest Ending

Doing the Math: A Small Town Romance

Daylight Delight: A Valentine's Novelette

Series

Hailey Family

The Boyfriend Type

The Playbook

On the Clock

Take It

Happy Hour Hoe

Shift Change

A Flick Between Friends

Legal Tender

Naughty or Nice: A Holiday Novella

Before I Do

Brand New

Halloween Stories

Trick

Treat

Trapped

Crave: Reverse Harem

Crave 1: The Prelude

Crave 2: The Show

Family Ties

The Prodigy

The Prodigy 2: Rise of a Queen

The Fox

The Player
The Prince

Printed in Great Britain
by Amazon